KU-152-899

A ROMANTIC AFFAIR

Running her bridal shop Maddy Hope feels she's put heartbreak behind her. Yet she can't fight her feelings when David Reid returns from Australia, to buy her parents' hotel. And when an Australian girl browses through the wedding dresses — it's just one reason why Maddy can't trust David. When she risks everything to protect her family's interests, Maddy and David are drawn together again during a crisis. Now they must face past secrets to reach a new understanding.

HANNAH FOX

A ROMANTIC AFFAIR

ABERDEENSHIRE LIBRARIES

WITHDRAWN FROM LIBRARY

Complete and Unabridged

LINFORD
Leicester

First published in Great Britain in 2008

First Linford Edition
published 2013

Copyright © 2008 by Hannah Fox
All rights reserved

British Library CIP Data

Fox, Hannah.
  A romantic affair. - -
  (Linford romance library)
  1. Love stories.
  2. Large type books.
  I. Title II. Series
  823.9'2–dc23

  ISBN 978–1–4448–1467–5

LP

Published by
F. A. Thorpe (Publishing)
Anstey, Leicestershire

Set by Words & Graphics Ltd.
Anstey, Leicestershire
Printed and bound in Great Britain by
T. J. International Ltd., Padstow, Cornwall

This book is printed on acid-free paper

1

Maddy felt a warm glow of pride as Guy put the final touches to the sign above the door. *A Romantic Affair*, it spelt out in black italics against a white background. Large bay windows beneath framed wedding dresses of satin and lace.

'What do you think?' Guy called down to her, smearing paint into his fair hair as he stuck the brush behind his ear.

'It's great,' Maddy put up a hand to shield her face from the bright morning sun, and her grandmother's amethyst ring glinted in the light.

The motorists driving through the pretty market town might have noticed the attractive young woman on the pavement. But in the flow of traffic no-one would have registered the details of Maddy's expressive features, nor her cornflower blue suit, made to measure by Inez, the seamstress. And they certainly could not have guessed that much as she loved her bridal shop and her attic flat above, her real home lay elsewhere.

As Guy came down the ladder to inspect his handiwork, Maddy pushed open the door to the shop. At the chime of the bell Inez glanced up from the confection of ivory silk she sat stitching. 'How does the new sign look?'

'Really good,' Maddy assured her. 'He paints well — for an actor.'

'Actor — huh!' Inez flicked her long black plait over her shoulder. 'When did he last act in anything?'

'Well, there was that play in Manchester,' she said, remembering how she and Inez had driven across the Pennines one bitter mid-winter's evening.

Inez tutted loudly. 'I don't mean a show you've never heard of where the cast outnumbers the audience.' Her needle paused in flight as she leaned forward to make her message plain. 'I mean, when did you last see him on television?'

Maddy gave her an apologetic smile, unable to recall such an event. As she slid into her chair she felt a fresh pang of sadness at the sight of the newspaper cutting which lay on her desk.

For sale: well established hotel with fourteen bedrooms and space for further extension. Close to this historic town and within easy reach of the picturesque Derbyshire Dales. Private staff accommodation included.

There followed a photograph of the grey stone farmhouse set among rising hills, and her parents' telephone number for enquiries. *Hazeldene* had been in Maddy's family since before she was born. Over the years it had become known as the most welcoming hotel in the town, if not necessarily the most modern.

Maddy had an uneasy feeling that standards at *Hazeldene* were not quite keeping pace with other hotels. Guests didn't seem to mind. If anything they left feeling they'd stayed in the home of some very slightly eccentric relations. But Maddy knew as well as anyone that her parents were growing older. The long hours, the commitment, the difficulty of ever having a proper break all took their toll. Now they too were starting to recognise they could not go on forever and her father had placed the advertisement that week with a very heavy heart.

Maddy knew the hotel was only bricks and mortar. Just a building, not a living, breathing creature. But all the same, she so wished there were some way to keep it in the family. And, if she was honest, she felt a twinge of guilt whenever she wondered whether she should have stayed at *Hazeldene* to help her parents with their business, instead of setting up one of her own on the other side of town.

'The wind will change and you'll stop like that!'

Maddy jumped at Inez's voice behind

her. 'I was just putting some things in the diary,' she said shuffling the newspaper away into the drawer.

'No good brooding,' Inez told her. 'I'm going to the Copper Kettle to fetch a sandwich. You want anything?'

Maddy shook her head. 'I could do with a customer,' she sighed, watching Inez's progress down the High Street. On the opposite corner she could see Guy, returning the ladder to the *Farmer's Arms*.

The telephone rang out suddenly, breaking the silence. '*Romantic Affair*,' she answered, 'Maddy Hope speaking.'

'Hello dear, it's only me.' Her mother sounded as chirpy as usual although Maddy knew she would have been up since dawn preparing the guests' breakfasts. 'I wondered if you were coming for lunch tomorrow?'

Maddy frowned. 'Well, yes. Don't I always come for lunch on Sundays?'

Her mother gave a little laugh as though she was nervous about something. 'I know, dear. But I just wanted to check. And to . . . well, to warn you, I suppose.'

'Warn me?' Maddy repeated. 'What on earth do you have to warn me about?'

There was a sigh on the other end of the line. 'I know you don't like the idea of *Hazeldene* being sold,' her mother continued in a tone which suggested she was about to break bad news. 'But we've had an enquiry.'

'Oh,' said Maddy. This sadness was selfish, she told herself. She must think of what was best for her parents. 'Are they seriously interested?'

'Yes, I think so dear. And the amazing thing is that you know who it is.'

'Really? Someone local?'

'He used to be local — before he went to Australia.'

Maddy's stomach gave a sickening lurch and she couldn't trust herself to speak.

'You remember David Reid, don't you dear?' her mother went on. 'He emigrated with his family when you were about seventeen.'

'Sixteen,' corrected Maddy. And David just one year older. There was no chance of her ever forgetting that day. Imagining him on the flight to Australia had caused her a pain which was almost physical.

She realised her mother had continued speaking while her own thoughts were elsewhere. 'So if you come for twelve tomorrow, you can catch up on old times. All right dear?'

Maddy was quiet for a moment, wondering whether to say she'd just remembered another arrangement she'd made, but knew her mother would think that odd.

'Ok, Mum,' she said finally and rang off.

David Reid. She couldn't take it in. They'd grown up together. His father, a builder, used to do some work at the hotel. Maddy and David had played hide and seek around the grounds; gone to the same parties. She just somehow believed that she and David would always be together. A childish fantasy, she knew. But when he had announced his whole family was emigrating to Australia Maddy had felt shattered by the news.

An uncle had offered David's father the chance to set up a business partnership which was too good an opportunity to miss. Now, eleven years later, he was back. David Reid was back. And not only that — he wanted to buy *Hazeldene*!

A little while later, Maddy saw from the bewildered faces of Guy and Inez that her own expression must be a picture of despair. She hadn't even heard the bell as they came through the door, but now they stood bemused in front of her desk, both clutching paper bags from the Copper Kettle.

'We bought some cakes to celebrate the sign,' said Inez, breaking into the awkward silence.

'Sign?' Maddy echoed.

'The sign above the door,' said Inez

8

as though she was talking to a child. 'I bumped into Guy in the High Street and we thought it would be a nice idea.'

'Oh, it was. A lovely idea.' Maddy forced a smile, noticing the meaningful glance which passed between the pair. 'Just excuse me a minute. I need to pop up to the flat.'

She hurried from the shop and fled up the two flights of stairs to her own quiet rooms. Eleven years since she'd last seen David, and still he had this effect! She took some deep breaths, knowing she couldn't be away from the shop for too long without attracting further attention from Guy and Inez. A splash of cold water on her face refreshed her enough to bring some of her colour back.

'Sorry about that,' she said as she returned to her desk where the fancy cakes had been arranged on a plate beside a tray of tea. 'These look wonderful.'

As usual, conversation flowed freely between the three of them as they shared the tea and cakes.

Talk of a new restaurant opening in the market square. A film just released which they agreed they might see. Some gossip among the market traders about the engagement of one of the stallholders to another. But the delicious cakes had no taste as far as Maddy was concerned because her stomach was filled with butterflies.

The afternoon brought more customers into the shop. Some brides knew exactly what they wanted for their big day, having studied magazines for weeks beforehand. But more often they sought Maddy's advice about what was best.

'I never knew there were so many shades of white,' marvelled one, surveying the racks of dresses which lined the shop.

It brought some light relief to Maddy to discuss the merits of ivory satin compared with cream, to shake out the dresses, and chat about the wedding plans with the friends, sisters and mothers who came in along with the brides-to-be. By five o'clock *A Romantic Affair* had done a satisfying amount of business.

'Fancy a drink across the road?' asked Inez as she pulled on her jacket.

Maddy shook her head. Any other Saturday night she'd have said yes, but not tonight. Tonight she had to be alone. 'Thanks Inez, but I need to do some preparation for that bridal fair next weekend.'

'All work and no play,' warned Inez. 'You can't spend every day selling wedding dresses to other people, then every night cooped up in that flat on your own.'

'I don't spend every night cooped up in the flat! You know I go out with my old college friends every so often. And I see you and Guy. And the family.'

'Well, if you're sure,' shrugged Inez. 'I'm meeting up with the girls from the flower shop later though, in case you change your mind.

Maddy gave her a firm smile as she closed the door behind her. She

11

dropped the latch and put on the chain. Work had served as a useful distraction since her mother's phone call, but now she climbed the stairs again with her emotions in turmoil.

Part of her had always been angry with David for leaving. It was wrong to harbour anger, she knew, but whenever she remembered how abruptly he'd disappeared from her life she couldn't help but feel that sting of pain.

Against her better judgement she brought out an old shoebox from the bottom of her wardrobe. Inside lay blue airmail envelopes, all the way from Australia. David's letters. How she'd pored over them when they'd first arrived, only Maddy knew. The tales of his first year in Australia burst from the page in his large energetic handwriting.

At first he'd missed England and his friends. But within weeks he was writing of new ones in Australia. Barbecues on the beach. Surfing. Maddy had hoped that his move would be temporary and he'd come back home to Derbyshire. But then David wrote about applying to university in Sydney. Maddy remembered how she'd felt left behind in every sense. David's new life had no room for her. For all she knew, she may never see him again.

By the end of that first year David had grown in maturity. Even his handwriting was more controlled. Maddy felt a single tear spill down her cheek. She couldn't read the last letter. She put it back into the box with the others and firmly replaced the lid.

She wiped away the tear. Crying wouldn't help, she told herself. It had been eleven years and David's life would have moved on — as had her own. When they met for lunch it wouldn't be as childhood sweethearts or even as friends. He would be the prospective buyer of her parents' hotel. Whatever her own emotions, her priority must be to smooth the path to a quick sale. Best to view tomorrow as a business transaction and not let any sentimental fondness for the past get in the way.

But driving the short distance to the hotel next morning, Maddy struggled to hold on to that cool perspective. She'd dressed carefully in a suit of olive green. Her hair was freshly washed and shining. Soon *Hazeldene* came into view behind the hawthorn hedge.

She parked next to a sleek black convertible. David's car, or a guest's? Her mouth dry with anticipation, she checked her reflection in the rear view mirror unsure of what she felt. Tense. Curious. Afraid. In all the times she'd dreamt of seeing David again, it hadn't been in these circumstances.

She walked briskly round to the back of the building where her family's living quarters were separated from the main body of the hotel by the second staircase. Jasper, their large black tomcat, sat on the paved pathway and she bent to stroke his warm, comforting fur. Straightening up she almost tripped over a row of hiking boots outside the door and she stumbled into the kitchen with inelegant haste.

'Hello, dear,' said her mother cheerily, looking up from the scrubbed pine table where she stood trimming the stems of pink carnations. Maddy glanced around to check David hadn't seen her clumsy arrival. Thankfully Mrs Hope was alone. Her hair was wound into a bun on the back of her head, the chestnut streaked with grey.

'Look at these lovely carnations David brought me,' she said. 'I'd forgotten he was such a considerate person.'

In spite of herself, Maddy gave an involuntary snort which did not go unnoticed.

'Are you all right, dear?' asked her mother, putting down the scissors. 'You're looking a bit pasty.'

'Am I?' Maddy tried to smile, knowing the importance of the occasion to her parents. 'We've just had a busy week at the shop. Are there many guests in?'

'A big family up from Nottingham, but they're all out at a christening.' Her mother filled a vase from a tap which spluttered and gurgled. 'Some more arriving tonight for the week.'

'So . . . where's David?' asked Maddy, turning her grandmother's ring around on her finger.

'He's in the study with your father. Going through the books. When they've finished you can show David round. I know he used to spend a lot of time here when you were both young, but I don't suppose he'll remember the details.'

Maddy sighed wishing she didn't remember the details either. David — the first boy she'd ever kissed, who'd broken her heart so easily. She shook her head, willing herself to forget. 'And are you and Dad really sure about selling?'

'Maddy, for the hundredth time, we are sure about selling!' Mrs Hope's laughter softened her exasperation. 'We're getting too old for this. I'd just like to celebrate our wedding anniversary here in the summer. Then it'll be time to say goodbye. Don't forget to remind your father it's pearls this year.' Her mother tossed her a striped apron. 'You can finish those potatoes while I lay the table.'

Maddy obediently put on the apron and picked up the knife as her mother sailed out of the kitchen with the flowers. She smiled ruefully. When David had left for Australia he'd bought flowers for her. A huge bunch of white tulips. When their heavy petals began to fall Maddy had replaced them with an identical bunch, then another and another, until it became too late in the year to buy tulips at all. Was this same man really sitting just across the hallway? Her hands began to shake with apprehension and she had to lay down the knife.

There was a movement behind her and a footstep on the tiled floor. 'Is that enough potatoes?' Maddy called out over her shoulder.

The voice which answered her was not her mother's but a masculine voice, as rich as chocolate and a note lower than she remembered it.

'Well, you know I always did like my food, Maddy.'

2

Eleven years might have passed but she would have known him anywhere. Hair as dark as her own, only with soft waves whereas hers was straight. The boyish look had gone from his face and his cheekbones grown more chiselled. But the same grey eyes met hers with a disarming intensity.

A wave of alarm overtook her. 'You're back from Australia then,' she said, all her rehearsed lines forgotten. She knew it was a pointless statement the second it escaped her lips. Of course David was back from Australia. Here he was filling the kitchen doorway with his solid presence, dressed in a pale blue shirt and beige chinos. And here was Maddy wearing her mother's old apron and with the dirt from the potatoes still clinging to her wet hands.

'It's good to see you,' said David, coming nearer.

'You too,' she admitted almost against her will. She hadn't wanted to feel like this, so churned up inside. Maddy swallowed, pride hardening her heart. 'Though it was rather a surprise after all this time,' she added crisply, seeing how David's mouth set a little more firmly at the sarcasm.

Just then her mother bustled back in, seeming not to notice the air of tension. 'Thank you for the flowers, David,' she said. 'They brighten up the dining room beautifully.'

'You're welcome, Mrs Hope.'

'Oh, call me Lillian.' She turned to Maddy. 'Now why don't you show David round before lunch. And take off that awful apron, dear.'

Fighting against the telltale pinkness she felt rising to her face, Maddy tossed the apron onto the table and breezed through to the ground floor of the hotel. Pull yourself together, she thought. You're an independent woman of twenty-seven with a highly organised life, not the silly schoolgirl you were when David went away. 'I expect you remember the layout,' she said in a tight voice, 'if you can cast your mind back that far.'

'Of course.' He brushed lightly past her, taking a notebook from his pocket. 'Naturally if I'd known you'd give me such a warm welcome I'd have rushed back from Australia much sooner.'

Maddy blinked in surprise. What was she to make of him? His tone was mild, but his eyes were hard and scornful. Who did he think he was, waltzing back into her life like this? Her mother might be won over by his easy charm and old-fashioned courtesy, but Maddy wasn't about to forget how he'd hurt her. Or to forgive.

'Oh, I'm so sorry,' she said with an artificial smile, 'if we'd had more notice we'd have hung out the flags and hired the town band to march past in your honour!'

Before he could respond Maddy

21

turned away to the rack of tourist information leaflets in the entrance hall. As a child she had been entrusted with the task of keeping them tidy, but now it looked as if no-one had the time. Chatsworth House was upside down. The Country Code mixed up with the sheepdog trials. She quickly rearranged the leaflets while David paced around rapping his knuckles against the wood panelling and noting the worn patches in the dark red carpet.

'I don't think you'll find any woodworm if that's what you're looking for,' she said.

'I should hope not — or any death-watch beetle either,' he replied. 'But you never can tell with these old places.'

'My parents have put everything they have into this old place, as you call it! They'd hardly let it go to rack and ruin!'

He gave her a doubtful look and Maddy felt infuriated. With her mother for putting her through this charade.

With David for his superior attitude. And most of all with herself. She hadn't seen him for all these years and within minutes of meeting they were bristling at each other like a pair of porcupines. Things weren't supposed to be like this.

Her spirits sank further as they entered the guests' dining room, for in the middle of the centre table was a fat marmalade cat. It sat content with paws tucked in, dozing in a pool of sunlight. This didn't look good, she thought. Cats on dining tables didn't look good at all. David had surely noticed but seemed unconcerned.

'Shoo,' she hissed, flapping at the cat. It leapt from the table with a disdainful glance, not unlike David's.

He jotted some notes on his pad and followed her into the main lounge, with its squashy sofas in slightly faded chintz. A grand piano half filled the room, a relic from the days when Maddy's father would play for the guests after dinner. Now though it was rarely used, all hands being needed on deck for more pressing tasks.

David lay a finger on one of the piano keys, and an off-key rang out. 'I remember this room,' he said. 'Weren't we banned from here when we were kids? In case we annoyed the guests? But you don't live here yourself any more, I understand.'

'No. I live over the shop — literally.' Her mother had evidently been chattering away to David, telling him all her business no doubt. 'It's called *A Romantic Affair*,' Maddy continued, challenging him with her eyes to make some smart comment, but he didn't.

So she went on to explain how she'd studied fashion design after leaving school, sharing a house in Manchester with three other girls. After that came a couple of years working in bridal wear until, with the help of a small legacy from her grandmother, she'd managed to open her own shop.

'You were close to your grandmother, weren't you,' remembered David. 'You must miss her.'

'Yes.' Maddy turned the amethyst ring round on her finger. 'But she was nearly ninety when she died. She'd had a long and happy life. And my parents still have her cats.'

'So I see!' laughed David, his face softening for the first time. 'I trust your parents will be taking them along when they vacate *Hazeldene*?'

Maddy gave a brief nod and looked away. When they vacated Hazeldene. It sounded so cold, and so inevitable. She perched on the piano stool while he prodded the wooden window frames.

'So,' she said dryly, 'however did you manage to drag yourself away from the delights of Bondi Beach?'

A flicker of emotion passed across David's face. 'My father died,' he answered.

'Oh, David!' Maddy's hand flew to her mouth in shock, instantly guilty. 'I'm sorry. I had no idea.' Her first impulse was to cross the room and take him in her arms, but her legs seemed rooted to the spot and she couldn't bring herself to move.

She pictured David's father, once captain of the local cricket team, and tried to absorb the news.

'It's OK,' he said as though sensing her awkwardness. 'It happened last year in fact, but we didn't come back to England right away.'

'Your . . . mother came back with you?' she guessed, not daring to ask if the 'we' referred to a family of his own.

He nodded. 'Mum's living with her sister in Cheshire, though she's hoping a house will come on the market around here. It was my father's dream to go to Australia, but after he died mum didn't have the heart to stay out there. This is her home. Mine too. My sister, Sally, stayed on in Oz though. She's married with two kids of her own now.'

'Sally's got children? That's incredible. I can only think of her as the little blonde girl in the front row of the choir.'

'Yeah. She's a teacher, and her

husband works in IT. They still live near my Uncle Jack.'

While they toured the hotel's maze of bedrooms and bathrooms David described the business his father and uncle had established in Australia. A small piece of land had grown into a leisure complex, the sale of which had brought in money for other ventures. Shabby motels were bought up and transformed. 'Both property and tourism were really booming,' he told her. 'We had no trouble selling our stake to one of the big hotel chains after dad died.'

'Really?' Maddy disliked the chill that ran through her. She would hate to see her old home being swallowed up by a chain, to become just another stopover for businessmen travelling between the north of England and the south. 'So what are your plans for *Hazeldene* — providing you bought it, I mean.'

David narrowed his grey eyes a fraction, looking pointedly at the frills and flounces of the bedcoverings. 'You know it all needs updating, Maddy. You can see that for yourself.'

'Yes, of course I can see that. But I've stayed in motels, David. They're all identical, no matter what town you're in. This place is cosy and it has so much character. Guests like the personal touch.'

'Don't you trust me with your precious *Hazeldene*?' he asked, raising an eyebrow.

Trust David Reid? She might sympathise over the loss of his father. After all, hadn't she too lost someone she'd loved? But trust him? That was another matter entirely.

She hesitated, intimidated by his closeness in the confines of the bedroom. The twin beds made it impossible for her to get out of the door with him standing in the way. 'I . . . we'd just feel happier about selling if we knew *Hazeldene* was in safe hands.'

'Your parents seem happy enough about selling to me,' he said with quiet determination.

'And do they know what you've got in mind?' she demanded. 'I know there's a lot of work to do here,' she continued wildly, 'but that doesn't mean you have to tear the heart out of it!'

'Maddy . . . ' He took a step towards her, raising his hands as if to take her by the shoulders, but she stepped back.

'Don't touch me.'

David buried his hands in his trouser pockets and moved to stare out of the window. Maddy took the opportunity to push past him and out of the door. She clattered down the first few stairs then forced herself to slow up. They had yet to get through Sunday lunch with her parents. What on earth would they think if she arrived downstairs so breathless and flustered?

She heard David's footsteps behind her but did not turn round. 'Perhaps we should see the gardens before lunch,' she said in a voice as icy as she could manage.

They walked in silence down the

path which divided the lawn in two. A small pond further on housed a family of frogs and a trellis covered in honeysuckle screened the vegetable plot. Beyond the fence the stream shone silver in the sunlight, threading its way to the river. As children Maddy and David had dammed the stream, flooded the vegetable patch and been roundly shouted at by Maddy's father. Despite herself, Maddy smiled at the memory.

She wanted to hate David. It would make things much easier. But how could she hate him, when once she'd loved him so much? He'd grown from the thoughtful, solemn-eyed boy, into this confident, almost arrogant man who talked with such an air of authority. And he was an attractive man too, though Maddy wished she didn't find him so.

She stood beside him, as he leant his sun-tanned arms on the fence and studied the rolling landscape on the horizon. He had outdoor hands, strong but not rough, and wore an expensive wristwatch on a leather strap. No wedding ring though, she couldn't help but notice.

Whichever way Maddy looked at it, her parents needed to sell the hotel so they could enjoy their well-deserved retirement. Did she want to be responsible for discouraging the one person who had so far shown any interest in buying *Hazeldene?*

'I really am sorry about your dad,' she said softly.

'I know.'

His grey eyes met hers and for a second she saw a remnant of the old David, serious and gentle. But then Maddy's mother called them in for lunch and the spell was broken.

The family's dining room had French windows to the garden and caught the sun, but like everything else at *Hazeldene* it had an air of faded neglect. The roses on the wallpaper weren't such a deep pink as they used to be. And there was an ominous crack in the ceiling. The snowy linen table-cloth laid with flowered china and the best silver cutlery was like a bright island in the middle of the room. David's carnations took pride of place, the cut glass vase sparkling in the light.

Maddy's father wore a fisherman's jersey and looked more like a light-house keeper than the owner of a hotel. 'Glass of wine, David?' he asked as they settled themselves around the table. 'Not Australian, I'm afraid.'

Maddy too held out her glass, thinking a drop of dry white wine was just the thing to steady her nerves.

David was laughing at her mother's story of how they had to dismiss the cook after a dispute over a missing ham. 'We haven't bothered to replace her,' Mrs Hope continued. 'It didn't seem worth it, knowing we were going to sell. A girl called Fran comes in on weekday mornings to help with break-fasts and do the cleaning. And there's Georgie — she's a student. She helps out in the evenings. But to be honest, we've been trying to keep the wages bill down.'

Maddy cringed with embarrassment, hearing her mother admit this. It was true that things had been hard lately. More competition and the relative cheapness of foreign holidays had caused a steady decline in guests at *Hazeldene*. But was it really necessary for David to see how much they were struggling just to break even?

'You see our problem, David,' her father was saying as he carved the joint, 'is that we can't start knocking the place about at our time of life. All the bedrooms should have ensuite facilities, which means the plumbing system would have to be totally overhauled.'

He laughed. 'I don't mean to put you off! But you're experienced enough in this business to know what people expect nowadays.'

David nodded. 'But if a hotel has a good reputation people will always come. The way forward is to guarantee quality. We have to provide all the comfort guests are looking for. Excellent service. A relaxing atmosphere. A first class restaurant.'

Maddy cleared her throat, not wanting to provoke disagreement. 'But the prices will go up, won't they — and then the regulars who've been coming here for years will stop visiting.'

'David's right though, Maddy,' her father broke in, evidently carried along with the younger man's enthusiasm. 'This place has a lot of possibilities. *Hazeldene* has to move with the times if it's to keep running as a hotel at all.'

'What do you mean?' asked Maddy. 'How could it be anything but a hotel?'

'Well just look at all the places that have been bought up for conversion to flats, or nursing homes,' Mr Hope went on. 'I'm sure we'd all rather see *Hazeldene* continue to welcome guests, even if there have to be some changes.'

Maddy gave a resigned sigh as David and her parents fell back into conversation.

Whatever he said to her father about

improving standards at *Hazeldene*, Maddy knew that once the contracts were signed the builders could troop in and do just what they liked.

'I'll be in touch about a survey,' David promised once lunch was over.

Her mother touched him lightly on the arm. 'It's been so lovely to see you again,' she said. 'Do call in for a drink any time you're passing. Maddy will walk you to your car.'

As ordered, she fell into step beside him, noticing how quickly he moved. As though he couldn't wait to get away from her.

'Look, I don't want to be at odds with you, Maddy,' said David as they came to the black convertible. 'It could make things very unpleasant if I decide to go ahead with the purchase of *Hazeldene*.'

Maddy shrugged as though the whole thing mattered not one ounce. 'It's all just business, isn't it, David. You want to buy. We want to sell.'

He didn't answer, but nodded as

though satisfied she understood the situation. Then he climbed into the car and swept off without a backward glance, leaving her standing alone.

Well, there we are, she thought. So much for the grand reunion with David she'd imagined so often. In the end, everything came down to a business deal. He was interested in her parents' hotel, nothing more.

Yet, what had she told herself only yesterday? To treat the whole thing as a property negotiation. Not to let her emotions run away with her.

For the next few days Maddy threw herself into work with a vengeance. It was months since she'd booked the stand at the bridal fair in the Town Hall, but suddenly the event loomed right ahead of her with still so much to do. With Inez's indispensable help the dresses were ready by mid-week, but there was still everyday business to attend to in the shop and a dozen little jobs to be done.

'We've got a fitting booked for

ten-thirty,' Maddy told Inez as they opened up the shop on Thursday. 'The one for the gold satin.'

'Oh, that dress was such a fiddle to take in. All that beading on the bodice.' Inez clattered around, getting herself organised for the day ahead. 'If I need glasses in the near future, I'll send you the optician's bill!'

'Hmm,' said Maddy, 'I don't know that I'd want to get married in gold.'

'Thinking of getting married at last are you?'

'No, of course not. I just mean that I like the traditional shades of white better.'

'Oh, right,' said Inez with a knowing smile. 'Well, people go in for all sorts nowadays. It keeps us in business.'

'True.' Maddy skimmed through the diary. 'I'll ask Janine to come and help you here while I'm at the bridal fair on Saturday. I was wondering if Guy wanted any work. I could do with a hand loading the van and setting up.'

'I'm sure he would. If his agent

hasn't landed him the leading role in some Hollywood movie, that is.'

Maddy laughed. 'I'm sure we'd have heard if he had.'

'You might catch him at the *Farmer's Arms* at lunchtime if you want to ask him,' continued Inez. 'He's filling in behind the bar all this week.'

'OK. I'll try and see him later. And if you're all right here for the afternoon I think I'll drive over to the printers as well and pick up those brochures I ordered for the stand.'

The morning flew by. The customer for the gold satin arrived with her mother and both dissolved into tears when they saw how stunning the dress looked. Even Maddy, who had witnessed this scene so many times, felt touched by their joy. This was the part of the job she really loved — sharing a little of that pre-wedding excitement.

Next there was a delivery of fabric to be checked which made the workroom even more cluttered than usual. Maddy ran up and down to the telephone, then just before lunch came another flurry of customers all wanting her personal attention. Not that she objected. The work was welcome and she knew it was better to keep busy than to dwell on her private troubles.

By one o'clock the rush was over. After a quick lunch of soup and toast Maddy crossed the High Street to the *Farmer's Arms*. A fine drizzle had started to fall outside, but the pub was warm and lively with chatter from the market traders. As she'd hoped, Guy was behind the bar with a checked tea towel slung over his shoulder.

'Hey, Maddy!' he greeted her. 'We don't usually see you in here at lunchtime. Is the stress of the bridal business getting to you?'

She laughed, pushing her damp hair from her face. 'No. I was looking for you actually.' She explained about the bridal fair. 'You wouldn't need to hang around all day. Just help me set up the stand, then come back later to collect the stuff.'

'Sure. I can still fit in a shift here as well then.'

'Of course! You are in demand, aren't you?'

He grinned and leant across the bar. 'And you know what else I've been offered? A week up in Yorkshire, as an extra for a detective drama!'

'Wow! That's fantastic, Guy.' She momentarily lay her hand on his arm in congratulation. 'Will we finally see you on TV?'

'You certainly will. Make sure you tell Inez. She thinks my acting's just a joke.'

'Oh Guy, I'm certain she doesn't think that. Inez is just a very practical person.'

Guy shrugged. 'Yeah, well. Maybe she'll take me a bit more seriously now.'

Maddy gave him a sympathetic smile. How funny, she thought. She'd never guessed Guy had quite such an interest in her seamstress.

Back outside, the drizzle had grown heavier. Maddy waited by the kerb for a gap in the traffic. Well, that was one job done, she thought as she watched the seemingly endless stream of cars. Now she just had to collect the brochures from the printers, organise the display for the stand, and do all those last minute bits and bobs which always seemed to get forgotten until the day of the event.

Suddenly a horn blared out, making her jump back from the road. The car pulled up beside her. 'Oh no,' she murmured to herself. It was that black convertible again.

3

The electric window slid open and Maddy found herself looking once more into the grey eyes of David Reid.

'Get in,' he ordered, leaning across the passenger seat towards her.

She stooped down to speak to him. 'What? Why?'

He pushed open the door and motioned towards her. 'Get in,' he repeated. 'We should talk, Maddy.'

'Well I hardly think this is the time or the place, David!'

'Maddy — I can't sit here all day holding up the traffic. And you're getting soaked out there. Come on.'

Honestly, she thought. This man. He disappears for years on end, and now he thinks he can barge back into our lives, take over the hotel, and tell us all what to do! She wrenched the door wider and climbed into the car, intending to give him a good piece of her mind. But next moment David had accelerated away before she'd even had the chance to put on her seatbelt. 'What on earth do you think you're doing?' she demanded.

'Maddy, we got off on the wrong foot on Sunday,' he said driving straight up the High Street and out of town. 'I know it was a weird situation, and we couldn't talk properly with your parents there too.'

'Oh, so you decided you'd come and kidnap me!'

He laughed. 'You still have to make such a drama out of everything, don't you, Maddy. I have no intention of kidnapping you. I just saw you there on the pavement looking bedraggled and so I stopped to pick you up — that's all.'

She shook her head in amazement at how presumptuous he was. And how patronising too. She didn't make a drama out of everything. Did she?

'I can assure you I didn't need

picking up, David. I was about to fetch my own car to go to the printers.'

David shrugged. 'That's OK. We can go to the printers afterwards.'

'Afterwards? After what exactly?'

'I was on my way to look at a house my mum's interested in buying. Thought you might like to come along and give me a second opinion.' He glanced across at her. 'Just one hour of your time, Maddy, that's all it'll take.'

She gave him a haughty glare. She should insist he stop the car and let her get on with her plans for the day. But they were already on the far side of town, and his car was certainly more comfortable than the long walk back to the High Street would be.

'One hour,' she said. 'And no more.'

David flicked on the radio to a jazz station she'd never heard of. He drove well, she noticed. Although of course, he'd had his first driving lessons on these country lanes. 'So,' he said. 'Let's see if we can't start again. Tell me how things are going with the sale of

Hazeldene. Is anyone else interested?'

'Oh, so that's why you picked me up! To find out about the competition?'

'No — blast, Maddy, can't we just have a conversation? You said we ought to be civilised about things, and that's all I'm trying to do.'

She set her shoulders back defiantly. 'Well, yes, since you ask. There's been a lot of interest.' In the hope that her fib would be forgiven Maddy crossed her fingers. Why should David think he'd have everything his own way? 'In fact, we've had a very good offer from a man called . . . ' the radio filtered into her consciousness. 'Ellington.'

'Oh yeah? Would that be Duke Ellington by any chance?'

'Don't be ridiculous,' she retorted, crossing the fingers on her other hand as well.

'He's a farmer,' she said as they passed sheep in fields criss-crossed by dry stone walls. 'But he wants to diversify.'

David's mouth twitched as though he was trying to suppress a smile. Maddy thought she'd better stop talking before she got into deeper trouble. 'So where's this house you're so anxious for me to see?'

'Not much further actually.' The deserted country lanes had given way to a small village of grey stone cottages set against a steep green hill. We have to turn left after the general store,' said David swinging the car around a bend in the road. 'Now we have to find the last house on the right.' He slowed down as they scanned the row of neat terraces. When they came to the end he consulted a leaflet from the estate agents. 'Yep. That's the one,' he said, nodding towards an idyllic little house which wouldn't have looked out of place on the cover of a holiday brochure.

'Oh, it's lovely,' exclaimed Maddy with pleasure. The detached cottage stood in its own square of land.

A rose rambled up the front wall and above the door someone had nailed a horseshoe.

As Maddy and David climbed out of

the car a portly man in a grey suit came through the garden gate towards them. 'Ah, Mr Reid,' he said, shaking David's hand. 'I'm Hugh Thomas from Thomas and West, Estate Agents.' He turned his beaming smile upon Maddy. 'And this must be Mrs Reid. How delightful to meet you.'

Maddy stared aghast at the man for what seemed like an eternity, then remembered her manners and shook hands. She meant to continue, 'actually my name is Madelaine Hope', but the man had already embarked on his prepared speech about how the cottage was convenient for village amenities, yet also secluded, standing as it did behind the pretty walled garden. 'But let's get in out of the rain,' he went on, leading them up the path. 'Are you blessed with children?'

Maddy remained speechless, but David answered quickly, 'Sadly not. At least, not yet.'

He looked at Maddy with a mischievous grin and she had a sudden impulse to kick his ankle for making her blush so obviously.

She would have to go along with it now. It was too late to announce she was not Mrs Reid after all.

'Perhaps you'd like to see the lounge first,' suggested Mr Thomas, directing them through a small hallway into a low-beamed room dominated by a stone inglenook fireplace. 'The owners have been letting out the house for some time, but have now decided to sell.'

He lowered his voice as though there might be eavesdroppers in the skirting board. 'Getting on in years, they are. But they'd be in a position to complete quickly if the right buyer comes along.'

David nodded. 'And the kitchen's through here is it?'

As they inspected the wall units with matching table and chairs Maddy realised she was beginning to enjoy herself. She'd always liked to look around other people's houses. It was one of the rare situations in which there was a perfect excuse for being some-what nosy.

'Are you a birdwatcher, Mr Reid?' the estate agent asked.

'No, I'm afraid not,' replied David with his usual courtesy.

'Pity. This area's excellent for wild-life. But perhaps you prefer more strenuous activities. Rock climbing, or sailing. You'll find both of those are available round here.'

Mr Thomas set off up the stairs, and David leant toward Maddie, whisper-ing. 'I guess he also has a job with the tourist board!'

'The bathroom has been quite recently refurbished,' said Mr Thomas proudly, as if it were his own. 'And through here is the master bedroom.' Maddy skirted the double bed and examined the built-in wardrobe. 'Plenty of hanging space, Mrs Reid,' the estate agent assured her.

'Yes, it's all been very nicely done,' she agreed, peering through the ward-robe door to the empty recess behind.

'There is a second bedroom across the landing.' The pair followed him. 'And as you can see the property has electric storage heaters throughout.' Maddy and David murmured appreciatively. 'I'm afraid there's no mains gas here though,' he added in apology.

'Well I think we've seen all we need to,' said David, descending the stairs. 'I'll be in touch in a day or two. When I've discussed things with my wife.'

They both shook hands with Mr Thomas and walked back down the path to the car. Once inside, Maddy put her hands to her face, which she was sure was still beetroot red. 'Oh, David,' she said in a cross voice. 'That was so embarrassing.'

He nudged her with his elbow and leaned closer. 'Fun though wasn't it?'

Maddy waved to Mr Thomas as David started the engine and pulled away. Yes, she thought. She had to admit it was fun going anywhere with David.

'So, Maddy, what now?' asked David,

manoeuvring the car past a tractor. 'Are you going to turn into a pumpkin?'

'A pumpkin? Why would I do that?'

'Well, you promised me an hour of your time and by my calculations that hour is almost up.'

'Really?' Maddie hoped her voice didn't betray her disappointment. 'I did have a million things to do, you know.'

'I'm sure. So if you want me to take you to the printers, I can do that. Or maybe . . . '

'Maybe what?'

'Take the scenic route. Grab a coffee somewhere?'

She thought for a moment. It didn't do to look too keen. But the prospect of another hour in David's company was hard to resist. 'OK then. Why not?' A thin mist veiled the hills, but Maddy knew the area well enough to see they were heading further into the dales rather than towards the town. 'So, where exactly are we going on this scenic route?'

'Stepping stones.'

'The stepping stones? In the rain?'

'I haven't seen them since before we went to Oz. A bit of rain's not going to matter. It'll be quieter in this weather anyway.'

Maddy pursed her lips doubtfully. At this rate they'd both be down with pneumonia by the end of the week. Really, this was turning out to be a very strange day. Presently they came to a small car park, empty but for a battered old jeep. 'I'm not really dressed for a country hike,' said Maddy, indicating her pale grey trousers and glossy shoes.

'Just across the stepping stones and back. Then we'll go for the coffee.' He went around to the boot of the car. 'Here,' he said. 'You can wear my waterproof.'

Maddy pulled on the oversized green jacket. The sleeves hung four inches below her hands and even with the zip done up the fabric flapped around her like a tent.

'Very glamorous,' he teased, pulling up his own collar against the rain.

'Come on. Quick march.'

'These shoes weren't meant for marching,' she muttered, slithering after him over a patch of shale. Despite his time away, David still seemed to know where he was going.

Two black Labradors chased each other along the river bank as their owner tried to call them back. Maddy stood aside to let them pass, wincing as a fresh shower of mud sprayed across her clothes. Another dry cleaning bill, she thought.

'Come on, Maddy,' urged David. 'I've waited a lot of years to see this spot.'

She tramped along behind him until they reached the stones. 'David, slow down. I'll fall in the river with these shoes on.'

'No, you won't,' he said, holding out a hand. 'And it's not deep anyway.'

'Oh that's very reassuring.'

She wrestled her hand from the long sleeve and let David steady her as they crossed the river from stone to stone.

Holding hands again, she thought, with her heart in her mouth. Holding hands as though nothing had happened. She expected him to release her when they arrived on the opposite bank, but he held on, pulling her closer.

He laid his free hand against her cheek, studying her face intently. 'Ever wish you could turn the clock back?' he asked, a note of roughness in his voice.

She could feel her pulse quicken. 'Turn the clock back?' she echoed. 'How do you mean?'

David nodded towards the river and Maddy saw the shadow cross his face again. 'In our house in Sydney, Mum kept an old photograph on the wall. Me and Sally, Mum and Dad. All lined up along the stepping stones. In happier times, as they say. No good wishing though, is it?'

Maddy frowned, searching to understand. 'But it sounds as though Australia was good to you. It sounds like you achieved a lot there.'

'Yeah, Australia was good to us. But

everything has its price.' He shook his head. 'Look, I'm sorry, Maddy. I probably shouldn't have brought you here. Too many memories.' He pulled away from her and set off towards the stepping stone.

'David, wait. What is it? We used to tell each other everything.'

He turned again, his expression unreadable. 'I really loved you, you know. I want you to believe that. Even though we were both just kids really.' Then he took her face in his hands and pressed her lips to hers in an urgent kiss that left her breathless.

A hundred questions flooded through her mind, but she didn't dare to break the mood. 'I do believe you,' she whispered.

He pushed her damp hair back from her face, the warmth of his fingers surprising her. 'Good. Now I think we should get that coffee, don't you?' He took her hand again and they crossed the river.

They found a tea shop, empty but for

a couple of cyclists sheltering from the rain. Maddy and David sat in companionable silence while the waitress brought them steaming mugs of coffee with walnut bread.

'Tell me about all those people we knew at school,' said David. 'What are they doing now?'

He listened while she told him who was married and with how many children. He laughed at her descriptions of all the unlikely jobs, the successes and failures, the snippets of gossip she'd heard. David was so easy to be with, she thought. This was how it always used to be, years ago. It seemed as if it would be such a short step back to those days of sharing dreams, making plans, talking, laughing, wishing.

He leaned towards her, covering her hand with his. 'It's been great spending some time with you, Maddy. Perhaps we could get together at the weekend?'

'I have to work on Saturday, but I'll be free by six or so.'

'I'll call you,' he promised. 'But now,

'we'd better get you to the printers.'

'Just drop me back at the shop,' she said. 'It's getting a bit late and I need to change my clothes. I'll fetch the brochures first thing tomorrow.'

As soon as Maddy walked in she saw how Inez gave a quizzical look to her mud-spattered trousers and shoes, topped off to perfection by David's huge waterproof jacket. Oh blow it, she thought. Why didn't I remember to hand it back to him? But then she had been distracted by the way he'd kissed her before she got out of the car.

'What happened to you?' asked Inez.

David Reid, Maddy felt like saying. David Reid happened to me — again! 'Something cropped up. Sorry, I meant to be back earlier. Why don't you go, Inez. It's quarter to five anyway. I'm going to lock up and take a hot bath.'

Once upstairs Maddy poured lavender into the steaming water and sank gratefully into the heat. She lay a long while in the bubbles, topping up the water from time to time as it cooled.

The real question, Maddy thought, was what had happened to David?

Something he'd experienced in Australia had changed him, that much was clear. Every so often she'd caught a glimpse of the shy schoolboy she used to roam across the hills with, but now he seemed an altogether darker, more complicated person. There was something he was hiding, she felt sure.

He could have any amount of secrets on the other side of the world. A wife and five children. A criminal record. Bankruptcy. An awful lot could have happened in eleven years. What had he said, about everything having its price? Maddy vowed that sooner or later she would find out just what he meant.

After her bath, Maddy went back to the box of letters. The last one, the one that was still so difficult to read, lay on top of the pile, the paper dry and brittle. Steeling herself for what she knew lay inside she slid it from its envelope. Jayne, that was her name.

'Jayne with a Y' as Maddy always thought of her. The girl David had met in his first week at university.

Though Maddy had been hurt, she wasn't completely surprised. A good looking man like David with his soulful eyes and English accent would have made a great catch for one of those Australian girls.

She wondered how long Jayne had lasted. Not that it really mattered. Knowing David had found a new girlfriend had been the end for Maddy. She didn't want to be 'just good friends'. She didn't want to read letter after letter from David, telling her about other girls he'd met until the inevitable one came announcing his engagement. Better to finish it quickly, Maddy had thought. And she'd told him so, in no uncertain terms.

'So much for the Australia fund,' she said to herself, picking up the old savings book from the bottom of the box. She'd never closed the account, though neither had she added to it in the last ten years. She smiled, remembering the invitation David had so light-heartedly issued.

Visit him in Australia, any time she wanted. So, as a sign of faith she'd opened this account and squirreled away a few pounds every week. Pathetic, she thought now. As if she'd ever have got to Australia on that! But although there had been plenty of times when she could have used the money over the years, for some reason she'd just let it sit there, gathering its little bit of interest.

And what now? David was back, and as far as she could tell they were both free and single adults. Being with him today had been like old times. He must still have some feelings for her, judging by the passion of his kiss. It couldn't all just be a game. Could she dare to hope that there would be a second chance to make things right.

4

The Town Hall buzzed with excited voices, as exhibitors set up their stands for the bridal fair. Maddy worked quickly, listening to the conversations going on around her as she decorated the table with white ribbons and bows. Business should be good, everyone said, now the rain had stopped. Two of the exhibitors squabbled over who had booked which stand, and the sound system sparked into life, sending the sound of violins floating through the air.

Guy, one of the few men in the room, wove his way through the hall to Maddy. 'Here's the flask,' he said, setting it down behind the stand. 'Now are you sure there's nothing else before I go?'

Maddy looked around. The brochures, which she'd hastily collected the previous morning, were fanned out across the table. She had business cards in a small leather box and a folder of fabric samples. Behind her stood the row of tailors' dummies showing off the wedding gowns in white, ivory and cream. 'I can't think of anything else. How does it look?'

'Well, I'm hardly your average customer, but I'd say it looks fantastic.'

'Really? There must be something I've forgotten. I've handed in the dresses for the fashion show this afternoon. So, all I can think of is to wait for the doors to open.'

Guy put his arm around her shoulders and gave her a comforting hug. 'Then stop worrying. I'll be back at four-thirty with the van. Enjoy yourself!'

Once the first customers filtered in the event began to take off. Maddy watched the hairdressing demonstrations on the stage opposite her. It was the lunchtime lull before she'd realised she'd gone a whole two hours without thinking about David. She thought he might have called her by now. But there were no messages on her mobile phone, and she could picture his big green waterproof still hanging on the back of her door, looking most out of place.

She wondered if his surveyors had been out to *Hazeldene*. No doubt her parents would bring her up to date with any developments when she went for lunch tomorrow. It was hard to believe only a week had passed since her mother's phone call brought news of David's return to England. Astonishing, how the world could be turned upside in just one week.

'Does this come in other colours?'

Maddy was jolted back down to earth by the leggy girl who had paused to admire a satin off-the-shoulder design. Maddy noticed how very young she was, and how blonde and how sun-tanned. The next thing that struck her was the girl's pronounced Australian accent.

'Only, my friend had something like this for her wedding,' the girl continued. 'But it was a kind of pale pinky colour.'

'Ashes of roses?' said Maddy.

'What?' The girl wrinkled her nose in distaste.

'Ashes of roses. It's a greyish pink. I'll show you a sample.' Maddy flicked through her folder until she found the right one.

'That's the sort of thing.' The girl fingered the soft material. 'Ashes of roses. What an awful name.'

Maddy bit her tongue. She'd always thought it was a rather poetic name. But she'd learnt to be diplomatic with her customers. Tact was a skill she'd acquired from her mother, in all her years of dealing with difficult guests at *Hazeldene*. 'Is it a summer wedding you're planning?'

'Yeah — next Christmas! That's summer where I come from.'

'Oh, I see. So you're looking for a dress to take back with you.'

64

The girl nodded. 'We're just wrapping up some family business. Then we're going back to Sydney — thank God! I couldn't believe how much rain we had this week. April showers, people kept saying, though it's nearly May.'

'Oh, England has its compensations,' said Maddy. 'Anyway, I can order the dress for you in this colour if you want to come in for a fitting.'

'You know, I'll just take a brochure. I've gone off being married in ashes of roses.'

'OK.' Maddy handed her a brochure and a card. 'Feel free to drop into the shop. It's *Romantic Affair*, on the High Street.' Was an odd coincidence, she thought as the girl sauntered away. She poured some coffee from the flask and settled herself down to await her next customer.

'Did you have a good day?' asked Guy when he returned.

'Yes, it was definitely worth coming. Although my feet are killing me.' Maddy packed up the dresses while

Guy pulled the yards of ribbon from the table and bundled it into a carrier bag. Between them they ferried the stock out to the van and back to the shop.

'Don't worry about where to put things for now,' said Maddy as Guy piled up boxes all around the workroom. 'I'll have a good sort out later.'

'It's Saturday night for goodness sake,' exclaimed Guy. 'You must have something more exciting planned than sorting out boxes.'

She glanced at the screen of her mobile. Still no messages. 'Well, let me see. I could choose between the Lord Mayor's banquet, a charity ball, or going to a film premier.'

'Ha, ha. Come over the road then. We can fit in a quick one at the *Farmer's Arms* before my shift starts.' Seeing her uncertainty he continued with his gentle persuasion. 'You deserve a drink after all your hard work. And perhaps Inez will be in there with those flower girls.'

Maddy chuckled. 'Oh, I might have known Inez's name would crop up somewhere. Come on then, Guy. Just one drink, mind. I've got this stuff to put away.' And she thought, there was still a chance that David would ring her. She'd told him she wouldn't be free before six.

The pub was busy, but there was no sign of Inez. 'Maybe she already caught the bus home,' said Guy, peering round the bar. He shrugged. 'Oh well, I'd just like to have seen her before I go to Yorkshire next week. You did tell her about my part in the detective drama?'

'Of course I told her.' Maddy leaned her elbow against the bar. She could hardly mention Inez's comment about it being time Guy found a proper job. 'You really like her, don't you?'

He gave her a sad smile and swirled his beer around in his glass. 'For all the good it does me. If she liked me half as much, I'd be happy.'

'Oh, Guy,' sighed Maddy, touching her hand to his arm. 'She does like you,'

'As a friend maybe. Women always like me as a friend. I'm just destined to be one of the supporting cast. Never the romantic hero.'

Maddy felt oddly moved by this. Why couldn't she have fallen for someone like Guy? Someone open and candid, who wore his heart on his sleeve. He was a handsome man too, tall and fair. And now she looked closely, his blue eyes were quite striking. But no. Such a straightforward course of action seemed to be beyond her. She'd had to go and let David Reid get under her skin.

'Don't give up,' she told Guy. The old railway clock behind the bar read almost six. She stretched to give him a peck on the cheek. 'I have to go. Thanks for the drink. And good luck for next week. As soon as you get back from Yorkshire you must come in and tell us how the filming went.'

She headed for the door thinking how nice it would be to take off her shoes after the long day. Then she halted abruptly as she recognised the couple sitting at the table by the exit.

David's eyes were already fixed upon her so there was no chance of making a quick escape without being seen. Meanwhile the blonde Australian from the bridal fair was jabbering away to David, oblivious to the fact that his attention was somewhere else. Maddy intended to give them a curt nod as she passed, but David was rising to his feet to greet her.

'Maddy,' he said. 'How are you?'

'Fine.' She glanced at his companion.

'This is Alicia. Alicia — this is Maddy who runs the bridal shop in the High Street.'

The girl's gaze focused upon then, then realisation dawned. 'Oh yeah — we met earlier, didn't we?'

Maddy nodded. 'That's right. But if you'll excuse me . . . '

Alicia continued talking as though Maddy hadn't spoken. 'I was looking for a genuine English wedding dress to take back home.' She reached up to tug at David's sleeve. 'And this guy here is going to pay for it.'

'Oh really?' said David, throwing Alicia a look of amusement.

'Yeah — since you're going to make such a killing on this run-down old hotel you're buying.'

Maddy blinked in shocked amazement. This was a nightmare. She had to get out of the pub, where she felt as everyone's eyes were on her, awaiting her reaction. 'I have to go,' she said hurriedly. 'Goodbye.'

'See you around,' called Alicia as Maddy bolted out of the door.

Not if I see you first, thought Maddy. She dashed across the street, her head spinning with her unexpected discovery. If she'd wanted a reason to hate David she certainly had one.

Only a couple of days ago he'd kissed her and said how much he'd loved her. No wonder he hadn't called. He already had plans for Saturday night with Alicia. Maddy had known he was hiding something. She hadn't expected that something to be a fiancée, right here on her doorstop. And what had that girl said, about David making a killing on some run-down hotel? That was Hazeldene she was talking about. Maddy felt so angry she could spit.

As she was about to step inside the shop she registered the sound of heavy footsteps on the pavement behind her. Startled, she turned. And then almost dropped her keys into a puddle.

'Maddy — wait,' he ordered, putting a hand on her shoulder.

'Go away, David,' she snapped. 'I've got nothing to say to you.'

He caught hold of her arm as she tried to throw him off. She glanced up and down the High Street, wondering which of her neighbours was witnessing this unprecedented scene.

'Let me go,' she insisted, wrenching herself free. He marched into the shop ahead of her, straight through to the workroom at the back. The bell clanged in protest as Maddy slammed the door.

On the wall Inez had stuck a poster of a fiesta in Mexico which she'd bought on a visit to some distant relative. It made a splash of vivid reds and blues among all the ghostly white satin. David stood looking at it, his back to Maddy.

'Well?' she demanded.

'Do you suppose,' he said levelly, 'that dressmakers in Mexico have pictures of England on their walls?'

'How on earth should I know? I shouldn't think you've forced your way in here to discuss interior design.'

'No,' he agreed.

'Then what do you want, David,' she continued in a fury. 'To rub my nose in how you've come back home with your pockets full of money and a fiancée in tow? Or how you planned to rip off my parents and ruin the business they've built up so you can make a fat profit?'

'Don't be ridiculous, Maddy,' he said, turning to look at her. 'There are some things I wanted to explain.'

'Explain, David? Or tell me more lies?'

'I've never lied to you,' he said with indignation.

'Hah! Well you did a good job of not telling me the whole truth. You should go into politics, David.' She tossed back her hair. 'Of course, you wouldn't have wanted to mention Alicia over lunch last Sunday would you? That might have upset your business negotiations.'

Hid eyes darkened. 'It's not like that.'

She gave a hollow laugh. 'Oh no? At least your Alicia doesn't have any illusions about you. She can see you for the shark that you are.'

David shook his head. 'You've got this all wrong, Maddy. She's not my Alicia, as you put it. And she doesn't understand the business.'

'Oh, I think she understands very well. You want to — what did she say? Make a killing on a run-down hotel. That being *Hazeldene*, I presume. And then apparently you'll go back to Australia for your Christmas wedding to her. When only this week you were kissing me and asking me out. How could you, David?'

'As I recall, Maddy, we kissed each

other. You didn't fight me off. So don't put on this outraged act.' He crossed the room in a couple of strides. Instinctively Maddy took a step back, stumbled over a box Guy had left there earlier and sent one of the tailor's dummies crashing to the floor. 'And as for my private life — well what's it to you?' he went on. 'You were all over that man in the pub.'

'I certainly was not. Guy's . . . ' She stopped herself, remembering Guy's words about women only ever seeing him as a friend. Why give David the satisfaction of knowing the truth? 'Oh, think what you like. I should have learnt by now that you couldn't be trusted.'

He leaned across the worktable towards her, fingers splayed. 'And what's that supposed to mean?'

'Talk about history repeating itself. You went off to Australia at a moment's notice, telling me nothing until it was too late to talk.' She felt her voice rising and struggled to keep her emotions in

74

check. 'I don't like the way you treat people, David.'

'Let's not drag up that old argument. It was my Dad's dream to go to Australia. He sold the business so we could all go — as a family. I couldn't let him down.'

'But you didn't mind letting me down,' she said with less anger and more of the sadness that had been eating away at her for so long. 'You led me to believe you'd be coming back.'

'Well, yes. If it hadn't worked out within a year or so, we'd have come back. But I didn't expect you to wait around for me. That's why we decided we'd be just good friends.'

'You decided, David. I had enough good friends already,' she replied coldly.

He glared back at her, his lip curling in an ugly sneer. 'You must have a very dull life, saving up all this bitterness from the past, just waiting for the moment you could throw it in my face.'

'Oh, don't flatter yourself. I've been perfectly happy all this time, knowing that you were on the other side of the world. Why couldn't you have stayed there?'

David flinched. Because of his father, Maddy remembered, but it was too late to take back the words.

'I don't have to justify myself to you,' he said. 'If *Hazeldene* hadn't been up for sale we may never even have met again.'

'Oh, yes, *Hazeldene*. It all comes back to that doesn't it. Well I'm telling you once and for all David, if you get your hand on my parents' hotel it'll be over my dead body!'

She anticipated a fresh blast of anger, but it didn't come. David's expression grew distant and hard. He threw open the shop door, letting the rain blow in.

'We'll see,' he muttered darkly and strode off.

Maddy raced up the two flights of stairs and grabbed the green waterproof from the back of her door. Without thinking what she was doing she flung open her window, as David was waiting to cross the road.

'Hey, David!' she shouted. 'Don't forget your jacket!'

And with all the force she could muster she hurled the jacket out of the window, to land in a crumpled heap on the pavement below. Then she banged the window shut, pulled the curtains together, and burst into hot and angry tears.

5

'So how did the bridal fair go?' asked Maddy's mother next day over lunch.

'Great,' Maddy told her. 'Though I think I might have caught a cold.' She had to find some reason why her eyes were so puffy otherwise Mrs Hope would begin to delve. Mothers had a knack of hitting on the most awkward questions without even trying, she thought.

David's pink carnations were lasting well. Still sitting in the glass vase right in front of her at the dining table. She'd like to pick the whole thing up and smash it against the wall. But it was bad enough that she'd thrown his jacket out of the window last night. Oh, why had she done that? She felt ashamed of herself. As if she needed to give him another excuse to call her dramatic.

In spite of all this, Maddy had also

found her anger strangely liberating. She certainly knew where she stood with David now. A potential victim of his latest money-grabbing scheme. But she didn't have to go along with his plotting. If she sat back and watched helplessly as he took over *Hazeldene*, that would be exactly what he wanted.

'Has anyone else shown interest in the sale?' she asked her father.

'There's a chap coming to view on Thursday. Name of Harkisson. Don't know anything about him.' Her father looked tired, as though he'd had too many nights broken by worry.

'Well, that's good isn't it? Another possible buyer. You could always advertise more widely — or on the Internet perhaps.'

'We'll see if we get any local offers first. To be honest, we'd rather sell to David. But we haven't heard from him about whether he wants to arrange that survey. He's taking his time over it.'

'Your father was wondering whether to phone him,' Mrs Hope added. 'But we don't want to seem pushy. What do you think, dear?'

Maddy sighed. She didn't want to tell her parents that she'd warned David off. The whole sordid story would emerge and she would rather keep it to herself. 'Hold on for a few more days,' she told them. 'If you don't hear anything this week, I think we can assume he's changed his mind.' David could take as much time as he wanted, she thought.

A third alternative was taking shape in her mind. But she didn't want to mention it to her parents yet. 'What have you got planned for your wedding anniversary?' she asked to lighten the mood.

Her mother became more animated. 'Oh, we're going to have a big party out in the garden. We'll still be here then, judging by how slowly things are moving. We'll invite all our friends and everyone who's ever worked for us at *Hazeldene*. It'll be our farewell — but a happy occasion too.'

'That sounds lovely,' Maddy smiled.

She stayed long enough to help clear the kitchen after lunch, then returned to the flat. With a cup of strong coffee, a notebook and pen, she settled herself against the arm of the powder blue sofa. She scribbled down the asking price of the hotel on her notepad. It looked a huge amount of money, but *Hazeldene* was very well positioned with two acres of land. Maddy knew that the only way she could raise enough to buy her parents out was by selling the shop.

There were two options, as far as she could see. She wrote down a long list of figures, representing the amount that she could realise if she sold the leasehold and the stock separately. The total fell far short of the figure at the top of the page. Or, it might be possible to sell the shop as a going concern if someone wanted to purchase a ready-made business. Maybe that way Inez could be kept on. But the second column of numbers still didn't begin to reach *Hazeldene's* value.

She laid down her pen and perched her chin on her hand. The bank looked like her only other source of money. When she'd bought the shop she'd had to borrow to supplement her grandmother's legacy. But the amount she'd borrowed then was nowhere near the amount she was looking at now. She'd have to do business plans and income projections. Some sound advice was what she needed — and quickly.

Caroline Masters was one of the most successful people from Maddy's group at college. She'd owned a string of fashion accessory shops across the north-west before she was even twenty-five.

'So what's the crisis?' she asked, sitting opposite Maddy in one of Manchester's most fashionable bars. 'You said your bridal place was doing brilliantly when we met up at Christmas.'

'It was. It still is.' Maddy rolled her eyes. Where to begin? She couldn't believe how life looked so different, just a few months on.

Caroline gave a throaty laugh. She'd come straight from doing an interview with a trade magazine, and still looked immaculate in her designer suit. 'Well, something pretty drastic must have happened. You were very mysterious about it on the phone on Sunday.'

'I'm sorry, Caroline. I know you're busy, but I needed someone I could talk to. Someone I could trust, who isn't part of this messy situation.'

'Sounds interesting. Let's hear it then.'

Maddy took a sip of her drink. She outlined the briefest of facts surrounding the sale of *Hazeldene*. There was no need to broadcast all the personal details of her relationship with David. It was enough for Caroline to know that he wasn't to be trusted.

'So, you want to sacrifice a profitable business that you've spent years building up, and put yourself massively in debt to take on the hotel? And it's all purely to keep this David from buying it? If you want an honest opinion, that's crazy.' She leant forwards, looking Maddy hard in the eye with her searching gaze. 'That's not a business decision. You're letting your own agenda with David dictate what you should do.'

'It's not just about business,' Maddy agreed. 'And I admit that David and I have some history. *Hazeldene* isn't the Ritz, but it's my home, and that's the reason it's so important to me.'

'When we were at college, we all thought it was so glamorous, you having parents who owned a hotel. But do you remember when you invited me for Christmas that year and the oven exploded? I saw then what hard work it was. And what kinds of disasters you have to cope with.'

Maddy smiled. She well remembered the oven incident, and how the landlord of the *Farmer's Arms* had to cram in a dozen extra guests for Christmas dinner.

'Please don't be upset with me for saying this,' Caroline went on, 'I know you have a lot of emotions invested in *Hazeldene*. But it hasn't actually been your home for years, has it? If your ambition was to run a hotel, you'd never have gone away to college. You'd never have set up *A Romantic Affair*. It would have been the easiest thing in the world for you to stay at Hazeldene and gradually take over the responsibility.' Caroline sat back in her chair and crossed her legs, like someone who was used to being right.

'But you know how it is when you're young,' Maddy said. 'You imagine your parents will go on forever and nothing will change.' She touched her grandmother's ring, hoping as always that it might somehow guide her along the best path.

'I've left Mum and Dad to manage on their own. I didn't realise it was getting too much for them because I was too busy with my own life. Too selfish, maybe. So now I have to make a choice. I can see the hotel sold off, to David or to someone else. Or I can step in and have some control over what happens to it.'

Caroline gave an exasperated sigh. 'OK. I can see you're serious about this mad idea. So tell me more about this shop of yours.'

It was plain to see why Caroline was good at business, Maddy thought. As they talked, she spotted possibilities where previously none existed. One was for Maddy to live at *Hazeldene* and let the attic flat. She could convert the first floor into another flat and let that out too, since at the moment it was only storerooms and wasted space.

Of course Maddy would still be nowhere near the asking price of the hotel. But if she maximised her income from the shop, maybe there would be some scope for a partnership with her parents.

'Don't do anything without thinking it through,' Caroline said as they left the wine bar. 'Ultimately you know, the best decision is the one that brings you peace of mind. There's no point making a barrel full of trouble for yourself.'

Maddy laughed, feeling better than she had in days. 'Thanks, Caroline,' she said, hugging her. 'How did you get to be so sensible?'

What would she do without friends, she wondered. Men came and went. And sometimes came back again. But friends, they were for life.

At her mother's request Maddy returned to help at Hazeldene on Thursday while her father was tied up with Mr Harkisson. Mrs Hope greeted her at the door, looking unusually flustered and hot. 'Oh, Maddy,' she blurted out, with anxiety in her voice. 'I don't like these people at all.'

'What people?'

'There are three men in the study with your father. Mr Harkisson and another two who work for him, managing his businesses.'

Maddy frowned. 'What kind of businesses?'

'Well, they seem a bit cagey. They run some pubs or clubs up north. But we can't get a straight answer from them about why they're interested in *Hazeldene*.' She led Maddy through to the main kitchen, which looked as though a pack of prairie dogs had rampaged through it in search of food.

'I was so busy trying to tidy up before Mr Harkisson came that I just threw the breakfast things into the cupboards and now everything's in the wrong place. Could you sort it out for me, dear, and have a clean? We have six guests arriving this afternoon, Fran's gone off poorly and David will be here before we know it.'

Maddy froze mid-way through opening the cutlery drawer to put away the washing up. 'You didn't say David was coming.'

'Didn't I? Well, he's bringing a surveyor over, around one o'clock. Let's hope Mr Harkisson's lot have gone by then.'

On a better day, she'd have accused

her mother of matchmaking, but that wouldn't help matters. She'd hide in the kitchen, Maddy thought. She couldn't face him again, not after their argument. And the nerve of the man — turning up with a surveyor just days after that awful scene at the shop. Why didn't he have the grace to bow out of the battle for *Hazeldene*? It was almost as if he was taunting her.

'Why David's sudden rush to bring a surveyor round?' she asked. 'Dad said he was dragging his feet.'

'I don't know, dear,' her mother sighed. 'I just pray that it's all settled soon. We'll have to take the best offer we can get, whoever it's from.'

Maddy took a breath to steady herself. Things were moving more quickly than she'd anticipated. All the more reason to press on with her plans. 'And what if the best offer came from me?'

'You? What do you mean?'

'Look, Mum, I've been thinking. None of us really wants to see

Hazeldene sold off. What if I moved back in and helped you run the place? We could be partners. I could raise some money from the shop for the improvements.'

'Do you think we'd sell up if we could see another way round the problem? It's kind of you to offer, dear. But we're not looking for a partnership. I told you, we're too old for this. We're ready to put our feet up.'

'OK then.' She could almost hear Caroline in the background, advising her against the gamble she was about to take. 'What if I sold the shop and bought you out?'

Her mother gasped. 'But we wouldn't want you to do that. You've worked so hard, Maddy. Don't give up your lovely little place to take on this crumbling old wreck.'

'It's not a wreck, Mum,' Maddy maintained. 'I could turn this hotel around.'

'I know you could. Didn't we always tell you that you could do anything if you put your mind to it? But this is such a big task. Your dad and me, we've leant on each other to keep *Hazeldene* going. But you'd be run ragged, trying to do everything by yourself.'

'Will you discuss it with Dad, at least? I'll have to go in an hour. Inez is on her own and there are a couple of fittings booked. Please, Mum. Think about what I'm saying.'

'All right. I'll talk to your dad about it later, if we ever get a minute to ourselves. But I must go up and get those bedrooms ready.'

As the door swung open, Maddy caught a glimpse of Mr Harkisson and his men, in the corridor with her father. The one she assumed was Harkisson was squat with grizzled grey hair. The others were young and slick. They were talking too fast, bombarding her father with questions. Perhaps she should go out and give him some support. But then it might appear that she couldn't leave him to handle the situation on his own. Better to keep out of the way, she decided. Hopefully, once her father learnt of her proposition, Harkisson would be out of the picture. And David too.

She turned her attention to the kitchen. She swept up the crumbs, returned all the half-empty packets to the correct cupboards, and scrubbed the worktops until the smell of bleach caught in her throat. Moving the rubbish bin, she thought she saw a quick flick of something behind. Something that looked like a tail.

'Oh no,' she whispered. 'Not a mouse. Not today.'

Mice didn't scare her. The cats were always bringing them in from the fields, often still alive. Her mother had developed a technique of rounding them up, involving a lot of patience and a large wicker sewing basket. But Maddy felt sure she could trust that mouse to pop its head out at the worst possible time. She couldn't tell if Mr Harkisson and his cronies were still there.

Doors banged and floorboards creaked around the building. That could just be her mother, darting through the bedrooms with fresh sheets and towels. She opened the kitchen door and peered down the corridor. Her father's voice came from somewhere far away.

She ran upstairs on tiptoes. 'Mouse,' she whispered, finding her mother by the linen cupboard.

'What? Where?'

Maddy pointed downwards. 'Main kitchen. Behind the bin.'

Her mother threw her hands up in dismay. 'Oh, my. What else can go wrong? Your father's still with Mr Harkisson at the back. And David's just pulled up at the front.'

'No!' Maddy rushed to the window. It was true. David's black convertible was parked on the gravel below.

'I'll fetch the sewing basket and try to corner the mouse,' her mother said. 'You go and entertain David.'

'Entertain him? How?'

'Just talk to him, Maddy, for

goodness sake. Fetch him a drink. I'm not asking you to do the can-can.'

They separated at the bottom of the stairs, Mrs Hope running to the kitchen, Maddy to the front door. She took a moment to smooth down her dress and recover her poise. 'David,' she said, letting him in.

'Maddy. I didn't expect to see you.'

'No, I don't suppose you did.' Her heart was racing more furiously than it had when she'd seen the house. Think calm thoughts, she told herself. She didn't intend to show David she was ruffled. She gestured towards the guests' lounge. 'Why don't you wait in there. My father won't be long.'

'I am a little early,' he said, choosing a squashy armchair between the fireplace and the piano. 'My surveyor should be here soon.'

'Oh, yes, I know all about that,' she said airily. 'You're not put off by the competition, then?'

'What are you talking about now,

Maddy?' he asked with a withering glance.

'As I told you last week, you're not the only person who wants to buy Hazeldene. In fact, we've had three people viewing the property this morning.'

A glimmer of a smile crossed his face. 'Oh, let me guess. Count Basie, and some members of his orchestra.'

'You think you're very clever, don't you? There's another person as well. Someone who's deadly serious about putting in an offer. So I wouldn't book that removal van just yet if I were you.'

She swept out of the room on the pretext of making coffee. From the far end of the corridor came her father, with a tall man in glasses whom Maddy took to be David's surveyor.

Hearing their voices, David came out to greet them. And at that very same moment, Mrs Hope appeared from the kitchen with her sewing basket under her arm, her free hand clamped firmly on the lid. 'Just a minor repair,' she sang, breezing off into the garden.

* * *

'Inez, you're a godsend,' said Maddy, arriving back at the shop after she'd restored order to Hazeldene's kitchen.

'Does that mean I get a rise?' asked Inez from behind a pile of silk roses she was stitching onto the waist of a dress.

Maddy winced. 'Oh. Well, we could discuss it. I leave you to hold the fort so often that you probably deserve one. But I can't promise.'

Watching Inez patiently sewing, Maddy realised that far from giving Inez a rise, she might soon be firing her. Up until now, it had all been theoretical. A wild fantasy to return to *Hazeldene* as its owner, not just the daughter of the house. But if her parents agreed that she could buy them out then there would be consequences for others as well as Maddy. She wouldn't tell Inez yet. No need to upset her when it might come to nothing. She'd let her parents talk it over in their own time and wait for their decision.

The rest of the day passed quickly. Maddy worked late, dealing with a mountain of invoices. She'd never fallen behind with the paperwork before and she reproached herself for neglecting it. This business with Hazeldene was taking up a lot of time and energy. David too, she thought. He took up a lot of energy. But not for much longer. A sale would be made. Someone would win and someone would lose. And Maddy wouldn't be on the losing side. She was sure of that.

Friday came and her eyes felt weary. *A Romantic Affair* was no less busy than the day before, with the amount of interest Maddy had stirred up at the bridal show. By lunchtime she and Inez were glad to pause for a sandwich from the Copper Kettle.

'Look what the wind blew in from the north,' quipped Inez as the door chimed.

It was Guy, bursting to tell them which actors he'd met on the set of the new detective series. 'I was only playing a man in a café,' he told them. 'But you don't know where these things might lead.'

Inez looked sceptical. 'So what will your next part be? A man at a bus stop? Or a man in a dentist's waiting room, perhaps?'

'Oh, Inez,' scolded Maddy, seeing Guy's dejected face. But Inez just flipped her plait over her shoulder and went to wash her hands.

'What does it take to impress this girl?' sighed Guy.

'You don't need to impress her. Be yourself. Make her laugh. She'll come to appreciate you.'

'I wish I shared your optimism, Maddy.' He sat on the edge of Maddy's desk. 'Anyway, how are things here? Any developments at *Hazeldene*?'

Maddy finished her sandwich and crumpled up the paper bag. 'There's someone called Harkisson sniffing around, but we're a bit wary of him. Seems sort of shifty. Apparently he has some sort of clubs further north.'

'Not the Harkisson with the string of nightclubs and bars around Yorkshire?' frowned Guy.

'Umm . . . Could be. Do you know him?'

'I know of him. A couple of other extras I got chatting to used to work in one of Harkisson's bars. They said he was a real bully. He has a high turnover of staff, and that's never a good sign.'

'I see.' Maddy sat back in her chair while the revelation sank in. 'And these bars, what are they like?'

'The girls I met worked somewhere that showed all the football matches on giant television screens. They said it was noisy and rough. And there were always fights breaking out.'

Her eyes widened in alarm. 'That sounds horrible.'

All through the afternoon Maddy had visions of *Hazeldene* being tarted up into a rowdy bar. Surely that couldn't be Harkisson's plan? Would there even be a market for that kind of place in this little town? The image filled her with such a sense of foreboding that she stuck pins into customers, dropped the phone and banged her knee on her desk.

'Honestly,' exclaimed Inez, 'I don't know what's worse. Having you here, or not having you here.'

'Sorry.'

She'd have to warn her parents about Harkisson. And if Harkisson was crossed off the list of potential purchasers, that only left two names. Maddy and David.

She was about to call the hotel after she'd locked up the shop at five, but as she ran up the stairs to her flat the telephone was ringing.

'Hello?'

'Maddy, it's Dad.'

She hoped he was about to say they'd agreed to sell *Hazeldene* to her. But it was bad news. The worst she could imagine.'

'Maddy, I'm at the hospital. Your mum's collapsed. Can you come?'

6

'My mother's been brought in,' Maddy gasped to the nurse at the Accident and Emergency department. It had taken her almost an hour to battle through the Friday evening traffic and find a parking space at the hospital.

The nurse tapped the details into the computer with brisk efficiency. She directed Maddy along a white corridor, at the end of which was a small waiting room with green plastic chairs. Her father was sitting with his head in his hands. As he looked up she saw fatigue etched into his face, making him suddenly seem much older.

She sank onto a seat beside him. 'Dad — how is she?'

'They've been doing some tests in there. Said she'll have to go for a scan.' He grasped her wrist. 'They think she might have had a stroke.'

'A stroke?' Maddy repeated, horrified. 'Oh no. What happened?'

'She was feeling woozy all afternoon. Just tiredness, I thought. But she passed out as she was starting on the evening meals. Luckily Georgie was there. She phoned the ambulance.' He shook his head, as though he was struggling to believe the reality of the situation. 'Why didn't I see sooner that she wasn't well? Perhaps I could have done something.'

Maddy squeezed his fingers. 'You couldn't have known this would happen. Is she conscious?'

'She seemed to come round a little in the ambulance. Started saying something about eggs. But she was very confused.'

'Well, if she's conscious and talking, maybe that's a good sign.'

Her father shrugged. 'Let's hope you're right. Can't do much but sit here and wait.'

Sitting still was never something that had come readily to Maddy. She got up to study the vending machine with its aroma of stale coffee, and tidied the pile of dogeared magazines on the formica table of the waiting room. Her father stared at the floor, as if trying to find answers in the pattern of the grey vinyl.

After what seemed like an age, a doctor appeared in a lilac shirt, with a bundle of files beneath his arm. Maddy braced herself, feeling her heartbeat quicken as she and her father both jumped up.

The doctor was young, but confident. 'It does seem as though Mrs Hope has suffered a slight stroke,' he confirmed. 'We're admitting her to a ward upstairs for observation. Her blood pressure is rather erratic. We'll do some further tests tomorrow, then we'll know more.'

'Can we see her?' asked Maddy.

'The nurse will show you the way to the ward. Please be brief. I know you're concerned, but Mrs Hope needs to rest. If she tries to talk you may find her speech is slurred, or that she's disorientated.' He looked from Maddy to her father, giving them chance to take in his words. 'It'll be a few days before we can assess any long term effects,' he added ominously.

'Thank you, Doctor.' Maddy's voice quavered as she spoke, but she knew she couldn't let herself fall to pieces. She walked in a daze alongside her father down another seemingly endless corridor and into a lift. Long term effects, he'd said. What would those be? Maddy could only imagine the worst. Her mother had always been such an active person. How would she cope if robbed of her independence; her dignity?

They reached the ward and stood uneasily by the nurses' station while Mrs Hope was settled into a bay. Monitors beeped around the unit. The telephone trilled. Nurses passed by, throwing them practised smiles of comfort as they filled in charts and fetched equipment.

When they were finally called through, Maddy was unnerved by the sight of her mother lying frail and sallow in the bed.

Her eyes were closed. There were no roses in her cheeks today.

Mr Hope patted his wife's hand, as if wanting to make contact, but afraid of disturbing her. 'We're right here, Lillian,' he said.

'So tired,' mumbled Mrs Hope. 'So very tired.'

Maddy and her father exchanged an uncertain glance. They perched beside the bed, not knowing whether they should talk or what to say if they did. Maddy thought of all the times her mother had complained about *Hazeldene* becoming a burden. Why hadn't she taken more notice?

Instead of seeing that her mother was under stress and giving her some practical help. Maddy had been preoccupied with the fact that *Hazeldene* would have to be sold. Selfish, she thought. She'd admitted as much to Caroline and now she saw it to be true. Watching her mother's breathing rise and fall, Maddy made a mental pledge. Whatever it took to make her mother well again, she'd do it.

'I don't like leaving Georgie on her own for too long,' whispered Mr Hope after they'd sat in near silence for twenty minutes, seeing the visitors filter away from the other beds. 'Maybe we should let your mother rest, like the doctor said, and come back tomorrow.'

Maddy nervously curled a strand of hair around her thumb. 'But what if Mum wakes up and wonders where we are?'

'She's in good hands. What can we do here? It just makes me feel helpless.' He blew his nose. 'She'd tell us to get back to *Hazeldene* and keep the old ship afloat.'

'Yes, I suppose she would.' She kissed her mother lightly on the forehead.

Maddy's father did the same. 'We'll be in tomorrow, Lillian,' he told her. 'Just get a proper night's sleep and don't worry about a thing.'

They navigated their way back out of the hospital to Maddy's car. 'Is *Hazeldene* busy?' asked Maddy on the journey home. 'We might need to cancel some bookings.'

Her father shook his head. 'We can't cancel anyone. It's well-dressing week. We've a party of eight ladies arriving tomorrow from a branch of the Women's Institute down south.'

'Well dressing-week — of course. Is Fran still off sick?'

'Your mother rang her this morning. Her back's no better so she won't be in for a few more days.' He stroked his chin thoughtfully. 'We'll need to get some extra cover. You have the shop to run, and Georgie can only do so many hours.'

They turned into *Hazeldene's* driveway. Maddy hoped that the guests had all found places to eat and wouldn't give her father any arguments. He shouldn't be on his own tonight, she thought.

There could be news from the hospital, and in any case he couldn't manage on his own in the morning.

'I'll drop you off here and pop back

to the flat,' she told him. 'When I've picked up some things I'll come and stop with you at *Hazeldene*.'

At her flat she threw toiletries and pyjamas into her overnight bag. The notepad still lay on her table, filled with her calculations of what the shop was worth. She picked it up and shut it in a drawer.

Dropping the bag into the boot of her car, she glanced across to the *Farmer's Arms*. Guy had mentioned that he was still doing evenings behind the bar. She ran over and pushed open the door.

The pub was packed with people glad to have come to the end of the working week. Maddy was relieved to see Guy's blond crop of hair bent over pulling a pint. She tried to catch his eye through the crowd waiting to be served.

'Guy — have you got a minute?'

Maddy. What are you doing here? Are you on your own?'

'Listen, my mother's in hospital. It's a mild stroke, they think. I'm going to have to stay at *Hazeldene* for a while.'

His face registered shocked concern. 'Oh, Lord. I'm sorry.'

Tears began to rise, but Maddy blinked them back. Guy's kindness seemed so heartfelt, that it almost made her feel worse.

'Thanks. But can you do me a favour? Could you let Inez know the situation? And if you're able to give her any help in the shop tomorrow, I'd be really grateful. I'll pay you, naturally.'

He waved his hand. 'Oh, I don't want paying. I'll do whatever I can.'

She drove back to *Hazeldene* along the dark lanes.

By the time she arrived her father had sent Georgie home, and was working out the bills for the guests who were departing the next day.

'Have to give them tonight for free,' he said. 'They've had all this disruption. And had to find their own food.'

Maddy skimmed the reservations book. Her eyes filled up again at the sight of her mother's tiny handwriting.

The Bakers had arrived on Thursday for a long weekend of hiking, staying until Tuesday. The Drews came with an elderly aunt the same week every year, leaving tomorrow.

The next name down was a Mrs Mortmain, head of the party from the Women's Institute, and alongside that, in even smaller writing, was a word that looked like poodle. Maddy squinted at it. Yes, it definitely said poodle. Dogs weren't encouraged at *Hazeldene* but her parents sometimes accepted them, as long as they were used to cats.

'I'm making cheese on toast,' called her father from the kitchen.

'Great.' Now Maddy thought about it, she realised she hadn't eaten since her lunchtime sandwich with Inez.

They sat at the old pine table, both subdued. 'You know, we really need to get this place sold,' her father said. He rubbed his fingers through his coarse grey hair. 'I don't know how we'll cope at all, now your mother's ill.'

'I'll help, Dad. We'll muddle through.'

'We've been muddling through for a long time, if the truth be told.' He laughed, but not happy laughter. 'You mum did say you'd been thinking of buying *Hazeldene* yourself. We were surprised, Maddy. We thought you loved that shop of yours.'

'I do love the shop. But I hated the idea of *Hazeldene* being sold to a stranger.'

Her father cupped his chin in his hand. 'Well, I dare say we could have worked something out. But it seems to me that you decided this in a rush. And a rushed decision is very often a wrong decision.'

Maddy pressed her lips together, thinking. From the moment she'd seen her mother, so pale and exhausted in the hospital, she'd known her fantasy of buying *Hazeldene* was just that — a fantasy.

Running *A Romantic Affair* was one thing. It was an established business and ticked along without too many problems. And Inez was so capable. But bringing the hotel up to scratch would be more than a full-time job.

Even if she persuaded her father to agree a price with her, she couldn't take it on at a time like this. Her mother needed her. And she needed her mother.

Once her choice was made, it would be final. But she had no doubts. What were bricks and mortar, compared with her mother's health?

'It's OK, Dad. I wouldn't be able to manage *Hazeldene* as well as look after Mum. She probably won't be able to do as much has she has in the past. I need to be here for both of you.'

He gave her a smile full of sadness. 'You're a good girl,' he said, laying his hand on hers. He fell quiet for a moment, lost in thought.

'I don't want to sell *Hazeldene* to that Harkisson. I've asked around in the trade and only heard bad things about him.'

'Me too,' Maddy agreed.

'I'm hoping David's still interested,

but he hasn't put an offer in yet. He seemed worried about the roof.'

'Can you blame him?' murmured Maddy, thinking of the spot at the gable end where the rain blew in whenever the wind was in the wrong direction.

'I did a lot of business with David's father. He always played straight; dealt fairly with people. I'm sure David's the same kind of man. Could you ring him for me? Tell him we can negotiate on the price, but we need a definite answer one way or the other.' He held her hand more tightly, pressing his message home. 'Will you do that for me, Maddy? Will you ring David?'

The next day once the breakfasts were done, the cats fed and the guests checked out, Maddy could delay her task no longer. She didn't deny that between David and Mr Harkisson, David was preferable. In a few months he'd be back in Australia marrying Alicia. And then he'd be out of her hair for good.

As her father set off for the cash and

carry, she pressed David's mobile number. If he didn't answer, she could just leave a message on the voicemail. But after two rings, he came on the line.

'Hello, David Reid.' In the background Maddy could make out announcements from a tannoy. It sounded like a railway station, or somewhere similar.

'David. It's Maddy. My father asked me to phone about *Hazeldene*. My mother's in hospital you see and — '

'Hospital?' he interrupted. 'Why?'

'Well, she had a stroke. But the thing is — ?'

Again he gave her no time to continue. 'Are you at *Hazeldene* now?'

'Yes, but David — '

'I'm in Manchester, but I'll be there as soon as I can.'

She hung up with a sigh. If he'd given her time to speak, she'd have said he needn't come dashing over. Her father only wanted to arrange a meeting. Typical David. Pushing his way in where he wasn't wanted.

She shrugged her irritation away and ran upstairs to strip the vacant beds. Once the sheets were in the washing machine, she took out three cheesecakes to defrost for dessert that evening, then dragged the Hoover into the lounge.

The ladies of the W.I. were sure to have high standards. She worked like a demon, pulling out the furniture to banish dust, expecting a spider to run up her arm at any moment.

Her father returned with fresh supplies, and looked surprised to hear that David was on his way. 'He must be keen, then,' he said. They shared a tin of soup before he went to the hospital.

Maddy hauled the sheets from the washer into a basket to peg out on the clothesline in the garden. But as she stepped down from the kitchen door her ankle twisted on the Bakers' hiking boots, lined up in a row outside. She staggered, spilling the sheets out across the path as she landed on the ground.

'Oh!' she cried as the pain shot through her leg, making her eyes smart. She sat rubbing her ankle, shaken by the fall. Why couldn't her parents find somewhere else for guests to dry their boots?

'Maddy,' came a voice. 'Are you all right?'

She looked up to see David, frowning in bemusement above her. Trust him to turn up just when she was sitting in a heap of wet washing, feeling foolish.

'I'm fine,' she said, scrambling onto her knees. She grappled with the sheets as David stooped to help. He wore jeans today, with a darker blue shirt and jacket.

'And how's your mum?'

'The hospital said she was comfortable when I phoned this morning. Dad's there now. I'll go later.' She shook off his hand as he tried to balance her while she got back to her feet. 'They said it could be a while before . . . ' She broke off as her voice began to crack, and left him to carry the heavy basket of washing into the kitchen.

'Before?' David prompted cautiously from behind her.

The doctor's words still rang in Maddy's head like a curse. Speaking them aloud seemed to make them more real. But she forced herself to repeat the prognosis. 'Before they can tell how this will affect her in the long term.'

She turned to the sink and ran some water onto her hand where she'd grazed it in the fall. She heard David give a sigh of regret. 'Oh, Maddy. You must be worried sick.'

Had he put his arms around her then, she wouldn't have resisted. For a second she felt lost in fear. To be held securely in his strong arms would be so reassuring. But then she remembered the humiliation of seeing him in the pub with Alicia. She forced her attention to the view outside the kitchen window. The ginger cat leapt and turned in the air, trying to catch a butterfly.

If she allowed David a foothold on her emotions while she was vulnerable like this, he'd only hurt her again. Maddy dried her hands and pulled her cardigan tighter around her. 'You didn't have to come right away.'

'Well, naturally I'd want to be here,' she said. He ran a hand through his tousled hair, took off his jacket and hooked it on the coatpegs beside the door, as if it was already his very own kitchen.

Which, in a way, Maddy supposed it was.

'To get everything signed and sealed, so you can make your killing on *Hazeldene*?' she asked pointedly.

His expression changed from sympathy to distaste. 'This isn't the right time for settling scores, Maddy,' he muttered.

'No,' she agreed. 'We have a party from the Women's Institute due any moment. I haven't even made their beds yet. And these sheets will need to be washed again and hung out.'

'Surely you have a tumble drier?' he said. '*Hazeldene* isn't that far back in the Dark Ages.'

'We're not in the Dark Ages at all,' she bristled. 'My parents try to save electricity.'

'I think in the circumstances they'll forgive you if you use the tumble drier just this once.'

They both jumped as a loud 'Coo-ee' resounded down the corridor from the hotel's entrance. Maddy and David looked at each other in horror.

'I'll throw the sheets back in the washer,' said David. 'You go and welcome the good ladies of the W.I.'

She watched in amazement as he strode down the corridor to the laundry room. Had he always been this bossy, or had she just forgotten?

7

'Mrs Mortmain,' announced the woman waiting for her at the front desk. She had the air of a duchess who'd found herself in a setting less grand than she was accustomed to. 'We're rather early, but our driver seemed to think he was at Brands Hatch.'

Maddy put on her most welcoming smile, wondering if the woman always wore so much make-up in the daytime. 'Lovely to meet you. And your delightful poodle,' she added, glancing at the curly black dog at Mrs Mortmain's feet. 'I'm afraid your rooms aren't quite ready. But if you'd like to sit in the lounge, I can bring you some tea while you wait.

Mrs Mortmain's mouth set into a curve of disapproval. 'Oh, dear. We've been squashed like sardines in that minibus. I was looking forward to freshening up.'

'I'm so sorry. It won't take long for me to make the beds.' Maddy decided she may as well throw herself on the woman's mercy. 'My mother's in hospital, you see, and my father's gone to visit. To be honest, I'm a bit behind with things.'

Mrs Mortmain pursed her lips. Her sharp eyes sized up Maddy, who held out the register. 'And where is the linen cupboard?' she demanded, taking the pen and signing her name with quick distinctive flourish.

'I beg your pardon?'

The woman's features rearranged themselves into a pragmatic smile. 'Show me the linen cupboard and go and make the tea,' she ordered.

Maddy arched an eyebrow. Mrs Mortmain would be a good match for David. She didn't know which of them was bossier. By the time Maddy had laid out a tray of tea in the lounge, Mrs Mortmain had galvanised her ladies into carrying their cases upstairs and making their own beds.

She found David in the laundry, jabbing at the buttons of the washer, which wouldn't start. 'Dad should be back in an hour or two,' she told him. 'He wants to finalise the sale, and he's giving you first option.' Maddy pulled her hair back from her face, trying to regain control of the situation. 'Look, will you stop messing around with that machine, David.'

He turned towards her, hitching his thumbs into the pockets of his jeans. 'Only trying to help,' he said affronted.

'We don't need your help. Dad just wanted a firm answer from you about *Hazeldene*.' She glared at him over the washing basket. 'You've won, David. *Hazeldene's* yours if you want it. But you'd better not try to beat Dad down on the price, just because my mother's in hospital.'

'Your father and I will agree a fair price,' he said, a wounded note in his voice. 'Your parents were always kind to me when we were kids. Do you really believe I'd take advantage of the situation? What sort of person do you think I am?'

She shook her head. 'I don't know, David. Frankly, I have no idea who you are any more. And the only reason I'm not giving you a better fight over this is because of my mother.'

'Fair enough.' He fixed his eyes upon her so intently that she felt as if he could read all her secrets.

'Maddy, whatever our personal feelings towards each other, don't you think we should declare a truce?' He leant back against the washer, folding his arms. 'Your parents have enough to deal with already. They don't need a bad atmosphere between us as well.'

He was right. She knew he was right. Yet, could she really suppress all those feelings that bubbled up inside her every time she thought of him? The anger, the betrayal, the fog of confusion that wouldn't clear. She thought of her mother's ashen face in the hospital bed. 'OK,' she said finally. 'Truce.'

'Good. Now, why don't you show me

how to work this ancient relic of a washing machine and then go and lie down for an hour. It won't help your mother if you wear yourself out.'

'But I have to clean the bathrooms,' she objected. Already, he was telling her what to do again. 'And sort out what to feed the guests tonight.

'Maddy,' he said, more softly, appraising her with his dark eyes. 'You look done in. Take a break.'

She sighed. 'I suppose Georgie should be here any minute. She can do the bathrooms.'

'And I can keep the ladies of the W.I. company,' David volunteered with a flash of his winning smile.

Yes, she thought. I bet you're a real charmer where elderly ladies are concerned. She went to the washing machine. 'Just stop interfering with this and let me do it. You have to press the buttons gently, not stab at them.

Sleep evaded her, but Maddy felt better for resting on her bed for a while with a cup of tea. She couldn't remember when she'd ever drunk so much tea. She phoned *A Romantic Affair* to find Inez had everything in order. She'd sent Guy on an urgent mission to the wholesalers and her friend, Janine, from the flower shop was coming in to help for a few hours that afternoon.

What on earth would Maddy have done without Inez, she wondered. Now she knew she'd definitely be keeping the shop, she really must look at giving her that rise.

When she went back downstairs she heard a gale of jolly laughter from the guests' lounge as she passed by. David glimpsed her through the open door and excused himself. He followed her through the family's kitchen.

'Is Dad back yet?' she asked, pouring herself some orange juice from the fridge. She needed to taste something sharp after all that tea.

'No, but Georgie's arrived. She's preparing the evening meals.' David took the orange juice from her hand

and poured a glass for himself.

Maddy glanced at the clock. 'Isn't it a little early to start meals?'

'I told the guests we'd be eating at six instead of seven,' he informed her. 'It'll give you more time to get to the hospital.'

'Oh. Umm. All right.' She had to agree it made sense.

'And I've taken the liberty of asking Georgie whether any of her student friends might like to help us out here in the evenings.'

'Oh, yes?' Maddy noted the 'us', blinking at his blithe assumption that he was the one making the decisions. Could David rub it in any more, that he was near enough *Hazeldene's* owner?

'She'll bring her flatmate over with her tomorrow, so that'll be an extra pair of hands.' He closed the fridge door, and opened a packet of ginger biscuits that Maddy had left out on the side. 'Then I phoned Fran and asked if she knew anyone who could cover her shifts in the mornings, Her sister's agreed to do breakfast duties for now.'

'I see,' said Maddy crisply. Next he'd be telling her he'd put an advert in the job centre and trained the cats to do the cleaning. But she could hardly complain, since he seemed to have resolved their staffing crisis, at least temporarily.

The back door rattled, announcing her father's return from the hospital. His face was drawn and tense, but he brightened when he saw David making himself so at home in the kitchen.

David left off scrounging the biscuits and moved quickly to shake his hand. 'I'm sorry to hear about Lillian,' he said with feeling. 'Is there any change?'

'She's still very tired,' Maddy's father told them. 'But it could have been worse. She can probably come home in a few days time when they've sorted out some medication and stabilised her blood pressure.'

Maddy turned to fill the kettle, for the umpteenth time. 'Could you have a conversation with her today?'

'Yes, though she seems a bit bewildered by everything. She asked if you'll take her hairbrush tonight, Maddy. I'd forgotten to put it in the bag.' He gnawed at the side of his thumb thoughtfully. 'They said that although this stroke was a mild one, it could be a warning. She has to slow down, otherwise she could suffer a more serious stroke in the future.'

Maddy slid into a chair at the kitchen table as the implications of this began to sink in. She felt David's hand briefly on her shoulder, steadying her against the news. 'How are we ever going to get Mum to slow down? You know what she's like. She puts on a front for the guests; plays the perfect hostess.'

Her father shook his head. 'I honestly don't know. Even today she was talking about this anniversary party she wants. First Saturday in July, she thought. I don't see how we can manage that, with so much else to do.'

'Well . . . a party might be a good thing, mightn't it?' Maddy said. Her mother loved a party. Putting on a show; making people happy. That was what she was good at. 'It would give her something to look forward to. She could sit and do the invitations, and go through her cookbooks for the buffet menu. It would keep her occupied, without her running around the hotel all the time.' She seized her father's hand across the table as the idea blossomed in her mind. 'Let's do it, Dad. Let's throw the best party she ever had in her whole life.'

He looked back at her, a cautious smile gradually spreading across his face as Maddy's eagerness infected him too. 'Yes. Yes, you're right. Let's give her the best party *Hazeldene's* ever seen.'

They worked as a team on the evening meals. Georgie and Maddy prepared the food, David tackled the constant stream of washing up, while Mr Hope waited on tables. By seven the guests were settled in the lounge with Irish coffees. The ladies of the W.I. dealt out cards for a cribbage. The Bakers discussed local beauty spots and riffled through the tourist information leaflets from the rack in the hallway.

Maddy pulled on her fleece jacket and ran to her car for the trip to the hospital. On the ward, her mother was dozing in bed, the harsh lighting doing her tired skin no favours. She stirred as Maddy laid out the things she'd brought. A bottle of barley water. The hairbrush. A bundle of get well cards from *Hazeldene*.

'Oh, Maddy,' she murmured weakly, opening her eyes. 'Sorry to have given you all such a fright, dear.'

Maddy sat on the hard chair and took her mother's hand. What a relief, to hear her speak in her homely, comforting tone, even though she remained so pallid. 'Don't be silly. How are you feeling?'

'Weary. Old. Seems like a long while since I last lay in bed like this. I'm not used to it. But when I got up earlier on, it took every bit of energy I had.' She turned her fact to the window, where slatted blinds shaded the bay from the sun. 'I was watching those trees blowing about outside. And before I knew it, an hour had gone past.'

'Well, everything's fine at home,' Maddy reassured her, smoothing the pastel coloured bedcover and fluffing the pillow. 'You must give yourself time to recover.'

Mrs Hope sighed. 'I keep trying to imagine life after *Hazeldene*. Just doing ordinary things that other people do. Going to the cinema on a Saturday night. Having a lie-in on Sunday mornings. Maybe we can take a proper holiday — a cruise or something like that. It's a shame things have to change,' she went on, 'But, if nothing ever changed we'd all still be in the Dark Ages.'

Maddy suppressed a hiccup of laughter. This was the second time the Dark Ages had been mentioned today. She covered her mouth, pretending to clear her throat. 'I brought your hairbrush. Do you want me to do it for you?'

'That would be lovely, dear.'

Maddy carefully unwound her mother's hair from the loose bun at the nape of her neck. She smoothed out the tangled hair, seeing more grey than she'd expected. Whole streaks of it from her mother's temples down to her ears.

Brushing her mum's hair made her think of how her grandmother used to do the same for her when she was a little girl. When Maddy got too tall for her grandmother to reach, she was allowed to sit at the fancy white dressing table and her grandmother would do it there instead. It made her feel so grown up.

Her mother settled back, enjoying the rhythm of the brush as if she was one of the cats being stroked. 'Your father said David was coming over.'

Maddy stiffened slightly, but tried not to let her mother sense it. She and David had seemed to dance around each other like shadow boxers all day, each unwilling to concede a move.

Pretending to be friends. Making civilised conversation for everyone else's benefit. 'Yes. He's there now.'

'Good. David's a nice man.' She searched Maddy's face. 'Everything all right between you two, isn't it?'

'We're fine,' Maddy said. They'd declared a truce, hadn't they? But she avoided her mother's eyes, all the same.

The peppery smell of baked potatoes filled the air when Maddy returned to *Hazeldene*. Thank goodness, she thought. We'll have a proper supper tonight instead of living off tea, soup and toast. She actually had an appetite, encouraged by her mother's progress. But as she took off her jacket, David and her father came out of the study, grave and unsmiling.

'Something wrong?' she asked, fear beginning to prickle her skin. 'It isn't Mum, is it? She was OK when I left . . .'

'It isn't your mum,' her dad interrupted. 'It's that crook, Harkisson.'

'Harkisson?' She looked at him,

baffled. 'What's he got to do with anything?'

'He says I shook hands with him on a deal. And I didn't, Maddy. I swear it.' He looked at her, aghast, beseeching her to believe him. 'He made an offer on Thursday but it was way below the asking price. I said I'd consider it, but that was all. Now I've just had a phone call from him, threatening all sorts if I don't sell to him.'

Maddy tossed her car keys down on the pine table where they clattered against the fruit bowl. 'That's outrageous! We can't let him get away with that.'

David stepped from the shadows further into the room, his hands on his hips. 'I've told your father that we'll go up there on Monday and confront Harkisson in person. He might take more notice than if we just talk over the phone.'

'We?' she said warily.

'You and me, Maddy. You can represent your father's interests. And he needn't know who I am. I'll just say I'm a friend of the family.'

'That's right, isn't it, Maddy?' her father said, still seeming stunned by the turn of events. 'A friend of the family?'

She looked at the pair of them and forced a slight nod of agreement. A friend of the family maybe. But no particular friend of hers.

8

Two days later Maddy and David drove north from *Hazeldene*, watching the landscape change around them. Limestone became gritstone. The hills grew more craggy and bleak.

Maddy wore her dove grey trouser suit, fresh back from the drycleaners. She'd spent all of Sunday dreading her encounter with Harkisson, rehearsing what she would say to this bully of a man who was trying to swindle her father. In an attempt to project some of Caroline Masters' no-nonsense style, she'd scraped her hair into a French pleat and applied a layer of makeup to rival that of Mrs Mortmain. She hoped she looked like someone to be reckoned with.

Beside her on the driver's side, David wore a suit of navy blue, so dark it was almost black except for where the light caught it. He had his hair combed back from his strong-featured face.

Silence reigned in the car. David hadn't even switched on the radio to his jazz station. Things had been easier when they were back at the hotel, Maddy thought. Although David had spent most of the weekend at *Hazeldene*, they'd rarely been alone together.

Once word spread that Mrs Hope was in hospital, numerous friends dropped by to offer help and support. The landlord of the *Farmer's Arms* said *Hazeldene's* guests could each have a free meal at the hotel on Sunday night. Mrs Mortmain organised her ladies to take turns with chores. The atmosphere at *Hazeldene* grew quite convivial, as news came that Mrs Hope's condition was improving.

But here in the confines of the car Maddy felt tongue-tied. She and David hadn't discussed anything more personal than house prices or the weather in all the time he'd been at *Hazeldene*. He hadn't mentioned Alicia, and Maddy hadn't asked. She'd adopted an attitude of distant politeness, constantly guarding her emotions, and knowing their so-called truce was only for her parents' sake. His elbow nudged hers as he changed gear and she jerked her arm away as though his touch had burnt her.

She looked out at the shafts of sunlight slanting across the moors. Not far now, to the town where Harkisson based his empire. A knot formed in the pit of her stomach as they descended the hill. She gritted her teeth, steeling herself.

'All right?' asked David as they pulled up outside a snooker hall.

Maddy nodded, wishing she had a sweet to moisten her dry mouth. 'Is this it?'

'Yes. He said he'd be in the office at the back.'

'Did he ask what we wanted?'

David shook his head. 'I just told him it was a business matter.'

They walked briskly to the black-painted door and rang the bell. A youth, no more than seventeen, with a shaved head and earrings, let them in. The dark building felt so seedy that Maddy could imagine all the local villains doing business across the snooker tables. It smelt of beer and cigarettes and danger.

Maddy squared her shoulders as they entered the office, taking her first proper look at the man trying to cheat them out of *Hazeldene*. Harkisson was fiftyish, with a thick neck and malevolent scowl. He sat behind a mahogany desk inlaid with green leather, which looked at odds with the dingy room. He didn't get up as they came in, but studied them both from his jowly face, while a younger man stood behind him. His henchman, guessed Maddy.

'Madelaine Hope,' she announced with a show of confidence, holding out a hand for Harkisson to shake.

He made no move to do so. 'Miss Hope,' he said, his hooded eyes narrowing like a hawk weighing up its next victim. 'And Mr Reid, I presume.

To what do I owe the pleasure of your company?'

Maddy was determined to keep her voice level and her face expressionless, despite his tone of contempt. 'I believe you telephoned my father regarding *Hazeldene*.'

'Still trying to get out of the deal, is he?' He clasped his hands together on the desk, his heavy gold signet rings gleaming.

David stepped forward, but Maddy spoke quickly before he could butt in. This was one situation she felt perfectly capable of dealing with, inflamed by the injustice of Harkisson's insult. 'My father did not make a deal with you,' she flared. 'He's a man of his word and I won't have you intimidate him into accepting your ridiculous offer.'

'A man of his word?' Harkisson answered, twisting her accusation like a dagger. 'Let me assure you, Miss Hope, that your father promised *Hazeldene* to me. So it's him who can't be trusted.'

'I'd trust my father with my life,'

asserted Maddy, her dark eyes glittering. 'If he says he didn't strike a bargain with you, then that's the truth.'

'Then maybe your father's becoming forgetful,' he replied with malice. He grinned, showing uneven teeth. 'Perhaps my friend and I should pay him a visit to remind him.'

Maddy placed her hands on the desk and leaned towards Harkisson. Her anger blazed inside her but she had it well reined in today.

'If you go anywhere near my father, my family or *Hazeldene*, we'll have the police onto you for threatening behaviour,' she told him. 'No-one has a good thing to say about you, Mr Harkisson. Everybody knows about your sharp practices. Even your own staff call you a bully.'

'Who?' he demanded, becoming riled. 'Who said that?'

'Half of Yorkshire, apparently.' Maddy felt invincible now, and fearless. 'Whereas my father is known as a decent, hard-working man, who is respected by everyone who knows him.'

Harkisson sneered. 'That's probably why his business is going under. Decency might be very honourable, Miss Hope, but it doesn't pay the bills.'

She forced her voice into cool indifference. 'At least he hasn't ended up like you. Reduced to making threats and terrorising people to get what he wants.' She moved to the door, measuring her words as she gripped the handle. 'Don't forget what I said about the police, Mr Harkisson. And remember that you've made enough enemies in this world to put you out of business forever. It wouldn't take much for those enemies to turn against you.'

Maddy walked swiftly out of the snooker hall, sensing David close by at her shoulder. By the time she reached the car she realised her knees had gone weak. Her shaking hands fumbled to fasten the seatbelt.

'Phew,' whistled David. 'Impressive, Maddy.'

'Just drive,' she said. 'Let's get out of

this hellish place.' For Mr Harkisson had looked like the devil, she thought. Old Nick, in his black dungeon of evil.

As they sped up the hill, Maddy leant back into the seat. Once she could trust herself to speak again, they discussed whether they'd hear any more from Harkisson.

David was sure they wouldn't. 'He doesn't want the hassle, Maddy,' he said. 'Hazeldene doesn't mean enough to him to make it worth fighting for. He was just trying his luck.'

'I hope you're right about that,' said Maddy, allowing herself to relax by degrees. She shuddered slightly as she thought of how Harkisson had made her skin crawl. 'Thanks for coming anyway.'

He smiled. 'No problem. Though you didn't really seem to need me.'

But Maddy knew that having David with her had made all the difference. For once she hadn't let him get a word in, but his presence had made her feel safe. Next to Harkisson, David looked like one of the good guys. 'What an awful, awful man,' she murmured.

'Mmm. But you stood up to him.' He gave a quiet laugh. 'I almost thought you were going to throw his jacket out of the window.'

'Don't mock me, David,' she said coldly.

'I wasn't.' His hand reached across, brushing hers. 'Truly, I wasn't. Sorry.'

Her mood softened and she returned his smile. At least this was better than the awkward silence or the stilted conversations. 'I bet you didn't expect to get mixed up in my family crisis when you decided to buy the hotel, did you?' she said dryly. 'You'll be glad to get back to Australia.'

'Why do you think I'm going back?' he asked, puzzled. 'Everything I've done for the last six months has been geared towards getting myself established here. This is my home. I'm staying for good.'

She pursed her lips, figuring out what this might mean. Having braved the rendezvous with Harkisson, she knew she could tackle the subject of Alicia. 'So, are you just going back for the wedding?'

'Wedding?' David echoed, his eyes staring impassively at the road. 'Alicia's wedding? No, I'm not going to that.'

'How can you not be going? I thought you and Alicia — '

'I don't know where you got this idea about me and Alicia,' he interrupted. 'Shall we stop for lunch?'

He pulled off into a lane, where the hawthorn was just coming into blossom in the hedgerow. There was a pub up in the village ahead. A traditional, cosy-looking sort of place with a black and white exterior.

As David opened the door for her, Maddy felt his hand rest for a second in the small of her back. The imprint of his touch stayed with her for a long time afterwards.

'I'll fetch you a brandy,' he said.

While he was at the bar, Maddy went into the toilets to gather her thoughts.

In the mirror she still had the hard, professional image she'd put on for Harkisson's benefit. But she didn't feel like that person now, and she wanted to erase all memories of the snooker hall.

That dirty, horrible dive, run by such a horrible person. She washed her face and let down her hair. As she combed it through, it fell into waves from having been pinned into its tight coil.

In the lounge of the pub David had found a table and was casually flicking through a newspaper. He'd taken off his jacket and had his sleeves rolled up. 'You look more like yourself,' he observed as she joined him.

The brandy was strong and stung her throat.

Even after one sip she felt heartened, although she knew she'd probably pay for it with a headache later in the day. 'OK then,' she said, preparing herself. 'Who exactly is Alicia?'

David leant forward, resting his elbows on his knees. 'Alicia is Uncle Jack's stepdaughter,' he said. 'My step-cousin, I suppose, if you can have such a thing. Uncle Jack got divorced from my aunt a couple of years after we went to Oz. Then he remarried and gained Alicia.'

Maddy let out a breath which she felt she'd been holding forever. 'So, Alicia's getting married to . . . '

'A lad called Lee. Nice enough, but young. They're both young. And naïve. They've been staying with Mum and her sister up in Cheshire, sorting out some family stuff. Alicia and Lee went back to Sydney at the weekend. I was at the airport dropping them off when you phoned on Saturday.'

'Oh,' whispered Maddy as the clues began to fall into place. 'What sort of family stuff?'

'Just stuff,' he shrugged, not meeting her eyes.

His answer seemed rather vague, considering he now knew more about the workings of Maddy's own family than anyone else, but she let it pass. So, Alicia was never David's fiancée.

What a lot of heartache he could have saved her if he'd told her that before. Or, had he tried to tell her something about it on the night of their argument? Maddy couldn't quite recall, but her face burned at the memory of the way she'd raged at him.

David stared over her shoulder at the fireplace as though he had developed a sudden absorbing interest in the horse brasses. 'While we're on the subject, your boyfriend has been conspicuous by his absence the entire weekend,' he said, casting her a sideways glance.

She broke into hesitant laughter. What subject were they on? How they'd both misread the situation in the *Farmer's Arms*, with dramatic consequences? 'You're thinking of Guy, aren't you? He isn't my boyfriend. In fact, he has a serious crush on my seamstress, Inez.'

David nodded thoughtfully and went to fetch a menu. Maddy chose fish pie. David opted for roast chicken. They spoke little while they ate, both pondering what they'd learned. Piped music played in the pub. The usual selection of love songs and vapid tunes about loneliness.

The waitress brought coffee and Maddy solemnly stirred in the cream. She knew her priorities had changed since her mother's stroke. She'd relinquished *Hazeldene* to David, but that didn't mean she didn't care about its fate.

'David,' she began, 'you still haven't told me what you want to do when you take over the hotel. Will you just paper over the cracks and sell it on?'

'No way, Maddy.' He scratched his chin. 'I know it might have sounded like that, when Alicia came out with that stupid comment in the *Farmer's Arms*. But please believe me, I have so many ideas for *Hazeldene*.'

'But you won't stop at one hotel, will you?' she asked, scrutinising his face. 'You have too much ambition.'

David bent to examine his finger-nails, seeming reluctant to answer. 'No,

I'd want to have other projects as well. But not a big chain of places, like we had in Australia.'

'Perhaps there's a bit of your Uncle Jack in you. Didn't you always say he was the true entrepreneur of the family?'

'I don't have that much of Uncle Jack in me, I hope,' he responded vehemently.

'Why?'

David didn't answer, but drained his cup of coffee. 'Have you finished? Shall we get some fresh air? There are great views from up here.'

He stood waiting for her to put on her jacket, which after a moment, she did.

They walked out into the vivid blue skies and a scent in the air, which suggested summer would not be too long in coming.

Maddy blinked in the sunlight after the darkness of the pub. At the far end of the car park, a telescope was cemented into a concrete pillar.

David walked over and dropped a

coin into the slot. 'Hey, come and look,' he called, with a boyish enthusiasm for all things mechanical. 'There's a kestrel hovering over there. And you can see as far as the viaduct.'

'I've seen that viaduct a million times,' she said, leaning on the wall to watch tiny figures below weaving in and out of the dark trees on the riverbank.

Why did she have this feeling that David had arrived back in her life with his suitcases full of secrets?

If he wouldn't answer her questions about his family, maybe she'd try another one that had been bothering her for the last ten years or so.

'I know you'll probably accuse me of dragging up the past again,' she said when his money ran out and he stood up from the telescope. 'But whatever happened to Jayne with a Y?'

He threw his head back and laughed. 'Jayne with a Y,' he said with a nostalgic look that Mandy didn't entirely like. 'What do you want to know about her for?'

'Just to satisfy my curiosity.'

'Oh, Maddy! You have as much curiosity as those infernal cats. Jayne and I went out a few times. It was never a big romance.'

He grew more serious, moving to perch beside her on the wall. 'I wrote to you about her because I wanted to be honest. And I knew it wouldn't be long before you'd be going to college yourself, where men would be falling over each other to ask you out. You can't tell me they didn't.'

She lowered her eyes, not knowing what he expected her to say. 'Well, yes. I had boyfriends at college.' No-one recent though.

Setting up the shop had kept her so busy that it had felt as if there wasn't much of her left over for anyone else.

'Then I got your letter,' he continued. 'When you wrote that you didn't want to hear from me again, I was more upset than when Jayne skipped off with my roommate.'

Maddy gave a slight toss of her head

as though none of it mattered any more. 'I guess that's all a long way behind us now.'

'Since you and I are . . . umm . . . friends again,' he said, testing out the word, 'can I remind you that when we were at the stepping stones, you promised me a date?'

'And you promised to call me!' she answered in a pretence of exasperation, thinking of the times she'd kept checking her mobile phone to no avail.

'I was going to call you. But then I got roped into ferrying Alicia around. I was just sitting in the Farmer's Arms wondering how soon I could offload her when you walked in with another man.'

They laughed together for a moment, sharing the absurdity of the situation.

'I know things are hectic at *Hazeldene* right now,' David went on. 'And I'll help out as much as I can. But when your mum's back home and you can spare a few hours, there's somewhere I'd really like to show you.'

She gave a sigh, a sense of deja-vu

sweeping through her. 'Where? Is this another mystery tour, like when you dragged me off to see that house?'

'Oh, Maddy. Don't spoil the surprise.'

Maddy guessed he intended his smile to be enigmatic, but she just found it infuriating. She felt no nearer to fathoming him out than she'd been on that first Sunday when her mother had invited him to lunch.

'I don't know if I like surprises. I've had enough of them in the last few weeks to last me a lifetime.'

His face remained annoyingly Sphinx-like. 'Well, that's too bad. You'll have to come with me if you want to know, won't you?'

'OK,' she said at last. 'But not until life gets back to normal. If it ever does.'

9

When they returned to *Hazeldene*, Maddy's father was greatly relieved to learn that they weren't expecting any more trouble from Harkisson. They hustle and bustle of hotel life drew them back in. David continued to lend a hand with everything from cooking to repairing the fence when it blew down onto Mr Hope's cabbages in the night.

On Wednesday afternoon Maddy took the opportunity to call into *A Romantic Affair* on her way back from the hospital. Inez was refreshing the window displays. She had her black hair in two bunches, sticking out from the sides of her head. Inside, Maddy was surprised to see Guy, deep in conversation with a bride-to-be. They were sitting in the little velvet chairs, poring over a pile of wedding magazines. Inez grabbed Maddy's elbow and pulled her through to the workroom. 'Have to put him on the payroll,' she hissed.

'Really?' Maddy couldn't believe her ears. This was the first positive thing she remembered Inez ever saying about Guy.

'He's so good with the customers. All those hysterical mothers and overweight bridesmaids. I can't be doing with it. Half the time, I just want to give them a shaking!'

'I don't know if you should be telling me that,' Maddy giggled. She liked the emotional drama of the bridal business, just as she loved the frothy extravagance of the dresses. But she knew Inez liked to focus on the more practical tasks. 'So if Guy's here, you're free to get on with the sewing.'

'Exactly. He can do the patting down; soothing ruffled nerves. And give a man's opinion on things — which sometimes customers want, don't they? Not that we don't miss you, of course, for a gossip.'

'I hope I'll be back soon. My mum

can come home tomorrow, providing everything's all right when she sees the doctor in the morning.' She looked around the racks of dresses, realising how much she'd missed the rustling of the silks and satins, the soft comforts of the shop, and funny, sharp Inez.

She climbed the stairs to her flat to collect fresh clothes and water her plants. It seemed as quiet as a convent. Until she'd set up *A Romantic Affair*, Maddy had never lived alone. Growing up at *Hazeldene*, there was always someone to talk to. And at college she'd rented a house with Caroline and two other friends, so it had taken her some time to adjust to having a place that was all hers.

She paused on the first floor. She could see the sense in Caroline's idea that she should convert it to another flat. There were two good-sized rooms and it already had a small toilet and washbasin. Surely it must be possible to squeeze in a shower and a kitchenette. And in a flash she saw how she could reward Inez for her hard work and loyalty.

'About that rise,' she said when she returned downstairs.

'Oh, yes?' Inez stopped stitching and looked up expectantly.

Maddy explained her intentions for clearing out the storerooms. 'If you want, you could have the first floor flat, rent free.'

Inez pursed her lips and fidgeted with her gold hoop earrings. 'Is this just a way to get me to do unpaid overtime?'

'If you do overtime I'll pay you, the same as always. You'll just have to manage the gas and electricity. You'll save on bus fares too. And you'll be in the middle of town, if you want to go out with your friends in the evenings. Or with Guy, for instance.'

For once, Inez did not come back with a scathing comment about Guy, with whom she seemed to have formed an unusual alliance. 'How soon can I move in?' she asked, her eyes shining.

It was another week before Maddy

could move back. Mrs Hope was discharged from hospital without complications, but Maddy hadn't wanted to leave *Hazeldene* until she was sure her mother would heed the doctor's advice about slowing down.

The task of pinning Mrs Hope into an armchair with a pile of cookbooks hadn't been easy. But once Maddy's parents had agreed with David to close the hotel at the end of June, everyone concerned could start making plans. Mrs Hope turned her attention to searching the property pages for bungalows, when she'd finished the guest list for the party.

At *A Romantic Affair*, Maddy and Inez soon ploughed into clearing out the first floor.

'We should have known no-one would want this funny shade of yellow,' wailed Inez, dragging rolls of fabric from what would soon be her bedroom. 'And that pink doesn't sell well either.'

'Ashes of roses,' murmured Maddy with a wry smile. She rubbed the corner of the satin between her fingers. 'Can't we keep this one?'

'We'll never get finished if you want to keep everything!'

They heard the phone ringing downstairs in the shop and Maddy ran to answer it.

'Hi, there,' came David's mellow voice. 'Are you ready for the mystery trip yet?'

'What, now? I'm in the middle of a mountain of junk.'

'Tomorrow? I'll pick you up at ten.'

'But at least give me some idea of where we're going,' she begged. 'I won't know what to wear.'

A chuckle came from the other end of the line. 'OK. Well, to begin with I wondered if you'd mind if we called in on my mother.'

Although she remembered Mrs Reid from years ago, Maddy felt a tingling of nerves. It was a long time since a man had last taken her to meet his mother. But David had spent the weekend helping his mum move house, so it seemed reasonable that he'd want to check on her. 'And then?'

'Ah, Maddy. Be patient. You'll see when we get there.'

Was there ever anyone so maddening as David Reid, she wondered next morning.

He actually seemed to enjoy being elusive. Made a point of it, even. He'd said they were friends, but was that how he really saw her? An old flame, going out on a date with him for sentimentality's sake? Maybe he'd take her to another of their childhood haunts. She put on black trousers with a bottle green shirt and sensible shoes, just in case they ended up jumping across the stepping stones again.

'Going somewhere nice?' asked Inez as Maddy went out to David's waiting car with a bunch of tulips from the flower shop.

'Who knows?'

David was wearing the beige chinos and the blue shirt he seemed to favour. He raised an eyebrow at the tulips but made no comment. They chatted about the party plans while they drove out to the village. Mrs Reid's new house was just as lovely as Maddy remembered it. David nudged her. 'Hey, what about that estate agent marrying us off when we came to look round.'

Maddy feigned an ironic laugh. 'How wrong can you be?'

Mrs Reid opened the door as she heard them parking the car. 'Madelaine,' she said, reaching out to give her a hug. She'd changed her hair to blonde since Maddy had last seen her. The crow's feet around her eyes were white against her skin, from years spent squinting into the Australian sunshine. She took the flowers Maddy held out. 'Thank you. How wonderful to see you.'

'You too. Oh, you have this place looking so comfortable already,' said Maddy as they went indoors.

Mrs Reid made coffee and they sat together catching up on over a decade's news. David left them for a moment to answer his mobile phone and Maddy took the chance to study a photograph on the wall. She could recognise David and his sister, Sally, with their parents, lined up along the stepping stones as David had described. 'I was so sorry to hear about David's father,' she said.

Mrs Reid placed their cups onto a tray. 'David doesn't talk about it much, but he took it very hard. Especially with all that trouble over Jack.'

Maddy smiled as if she knew what the woman was talking about, and hoped she'd continue. But then David came back, saying his solicitor was pushing through the paperwork for *Hazeldene*. They took their leave, and set off north towards Buxton.

'Come on, David. At least give me a clue where we're going,' persevered Maddy. But he just carried on driving, staring at the road, with a trace of a smile at the corners of his mouth.

They came to an old country house with a sign that said Peakview Lodge Hotel. It was of a similar age to

Hazeldene but slightly smaller, built of the same grey stone, with a stone horse-trough and wooden half barrels of pansies beside the door. David silenced the engine and turned to face her. 'I know you're still worried what I'll do to *Hazeldene*. Bulldoze it to the ground and build a multi-storey car-park or something.'

'I didn't think that exactly.'

'Just come and look round. Lunch is included, by the way.'

As soon as Maddy walked in, she could see that Peakview was a completely different kind of hotel. The entrance hall was bright and welcoming in pastel greens.

There wasn't a dark wood panel in sight, nor any chintz, and the plush carpet gave softly beneath her feet. A chubby man with black hair and a moustache came out of a door, wafting the smell of home-made soup into the hall. 'David!' he cried, pumping his hand vigorously.

'This is my friend, Maddy,' David

said. 'And this is Archie, who runs Peakview.'

'Nice to meet you,' said Maddy, wondering why she was there.

'Everyone's out, so help yourselves,' boomed Archie. 'Here's a pass key.'

As Archie returned to the kitchen David led her into the lounge. A conservatory was attached, flooding the room with sun. The furniture was light oak, carved with leaves and acorns. On the walls hung watercolours of local scenes. Next they saw the dining room, furnished in the same manner. As they climbed the stairs she could still smell the freshness of the paint.

'Each bedroom is unique,' David explained. 'And they have the names of the dales, instead of numbers. This one is Dove.'

The room had the palest pink walls with a white iron bedstead and a small fireplace. The curtains were a plain rose, and the bedspread was a rich patchwork of Indian cottons in burgundies and pinks.

'Lovely,' breathed Maddy, awed by its air of luxury.

The next bedroom was decorated in autumn colours, named after Wolfscote Dale, and the one after that was called Beresford, painted a pretty blue.

'So, what's your honest opinion?' asked David as they reached the end of the landing.

'Beautiful. But why have you brought me here? Is it up for sale? Are you thinking of buying it?'

He shifted slightly. 'I already have. Half of it anyway.'

Maddy was speechless. She braced herself against the windowsill, staring at him in disbelief.

'I had to come to England for a few weeks last winter to start setting things up for me and Mum to move back in the spring,' he began to explain. 'I was looking round for a good investment and Peakview was on the market. Like your parents, Archie was faced with doing a lot of upgrading but he didn't really want to sell. I offered to buy a half share so he could stay on and bring it up to these standards.'

Maddy shook her head, still reeling. 'But why didn't you tell me before? All the time you've been at *Hazeldene*, helping out while Mum was ill, you never mentioned that you'd bought another hotel.'

'Half a hotel,' he corrected.

'Don't be picky.'

David looked down at the floor. 'I suppose I didn't want to scare you off. You seemed to think my intentions towards *Hazeldene* were purely mercenary. I thought if I showed you what I was trying to achieve, maybe you'd have more faith in me. Don't you like it?'

If Maddy hadn't been so cross she might have felt some sympathy for him. He looked like a child who'd just showed his favourite Christmas present to a friend, only to have the friend scoff at the new toy. She walked the length of the landing and back in an effort to calm herself. Archie was in the kitchen below and she didn't want Peakview echoing with their latest argument. She turned to David, who was still looking crestfallen. 'You must have told your mum not to say anything about this place when we went to visit.'

'Yes, I did,' he confessed. 'Sorry about that. But I wanted you to see for yourself, not hear about it second hand.'

'She didn't lie. And neither did I.' He straightened a picture on the wall, clearly not seeing what the fuss was about. 'Aren't you overreacting a teeny bit?'

'Don't patronise me, David,' she warned, her eyes blazing defiantly. 'My point is, how could you do it without saying a word? How could you hide a hotel up your sleeve? And don't say it's only half a hotel!'

'Big sleeves?' he said, spreading his arms in a Gallic shrug.

Maddy wished she had something to throw at him. Something soft would do, like a newspaper or a cushion. 'You always act like this,' she exploded in the loudest whisper she could manage. 'Whenever I ask a tricky question, you either make a joke or walk away.'

She saw how he winced, as though he knew it to be true. 'When we were young I used to think I knew you inside out. But now, you're so secretive. I never know how you feel about anything, or what you think. It's as if you'll allow me so far, but no further.' She hugged her arms around herself, unable to bear any more of David's mysteries and riddles. 'Take me home.'

He gasped and took a step towards her. 'No — Maddy, come on . . . '

'You call me a friend!' she said harshly, 'But you deliberately keep me in the dark over so many things. This place, your family, stuff that happened in Australia — it's all a big guessing game. Well, I'm not playing any more. Take me home and leave me to get on with my life in peace!' She turned to walk down the stairs, but he caught her hand.

'It was my fault dad died,' he said quietly.

'What?' She frowned, not knowing if she'd heard him properly.

'Dad — it was my fault.'

At the end of Peakview's garden was a flight of stone steps leading to the river. The water gushed over a small weir, into a deep, still pool where white ducks paddled. David walked outside, his hands deep in his pockets, shoulders hunched, with the air of someone who felt very much alone. He sat down on an old bench mottled with lichen.

'You're going to have to start at the beginning,' said Maddy, joining him. 'You said your dad had a heart attack. How can that possibly be your fault?'

David took a deep breath. 'When we first went to Australia, things seemed to be going really well,' he told her, tension creasing his brow. 'Dad and Jack got the business up and running. But after a couple of years, Jack split up from my aunt.'

Maddy nodded. 'Yes, and then he

married Alicia's mother, right?'

He cast her a rueful glance. 'I was away at university when that happened, so I didn't hear the full story at the time. Jack was a gambler, Maddy. I found out later that was why my aunt had left him. He didn't just gamble with his own money either.' He paused looking out across the pool for a moment. 'When Dad had his first heart attack I had to take on a lot more responsibility. I found Jack had been skimming the profits for years to fund his gambling.'

'Did your dad know?'

'Dad had always known,' he replied in a tone that shocked her with its bitterness. 'But he was Jack's brother so he covered for him. I discovered it wasn't only a matter of Jack diverting funds. He was taking bribes from contractors too, for giving out tenders for building work.'

'So what did you do?' she said, appalled by the dilemma in which David had found himself.

'I confronted Jack. Told him that we'd pull out of the business if he didn't stop. I wouldn't cover for him the way my dad had. It made me so mad to think of him taking advantage of us all.'

David's fair fell across his face, but Maddy resisted the temptation to push it back. She didn't need to see his face to know the pain that was in it. 'It was so alien to the way Dad had brought me up. He taught me to run an honest, fair business, not one based on bribery and deceit. I looked up to him, Maddy. He showed me how to live.'

Maddy stared down at her finger where the amethyst ring shone purple in the sunlight. She felt the same about her grandmother. She was someone who'd always guided her. Still did, in a way. 'Your father was a good man.'

He looked at her with gratitude, as though he was pleased she remembered. 'Yes. Well, I tried to broach the subject of Jack's gambling with Dad once he'd recovered. But he just pushed it away, like he didn't want to face what Jack had become.' He gave a laugh which was empty with desperation, shaking his head at the memories. 'Dad and I got into a huge row. I said I was coming back to England to start up on my own. A week later Dad had the second heart attack. The one that killed him.'

'But you can't blame yourself for that!' she said. 'Blame Jack, if anyone. He was the one who caused the bad feeling.'

He grimaced sadly, searching for the truth. 'For the last week of Dad's life the two of us were barely speaking. Family ties, that was all he'd say about it. But it didn't feel like we had much of a family left.' His voice was heavy with regret, as though what he'd learnt about life was more than he'd ever wanted to know.

'It's easy to look back and see where I went wrong. The mistakes I made. I should have been looking after things while Dad was ill, but I handled it all so badly. The past is gone and I can't change it. And that's a very hard thing to live with.'

She placed a hand on his arm. 'Your dad wouldn't want you torturing yourself with this. Your mum must have told you that.'

His eyes flickered over her face, gauging her reactions. 'Mum has her own grief to deal with. Jack's her brother-in-law and she's been trying to smooth things over. That's why she invited Alicia and Lee to visit and said we'd pay for some of the wedding costs.'

His crooked smile was at odds with the emotion in his face. He laid his hands on her shoulders, anchoring her down with the intensity of his gaze. 'So, who in the world would I talk to about it all, Maddy, if not you? From the time Dad died, you were the only person I wanted to tell. The only person I could trust to really understand.'

Maddy bit her lip. He looked at her with such raw vulnerability that she knew there were no barriers left between them. No secrets. He took her in his arms and she clung on tightly, wishing she could heal all the sorrow of the tears that filled his eyes. If she held him for long enough, perhaps she could.

From the garden of Peakview, Archie looked down. He'd brought out the old brass gong that he used to summon straying guests to meals. But seeing Maddy and David on the bench, he let his arm fall before striking the first beat.

It did his soul good to see their embrace. He knew David to be a kind, generous man, so deserving of happiness. And this Maddy reminded him of his own wife when she was young. He sent them a smile and went back to his kitchen to turn down the heat on the stove.

10

On the first Saturday in July the scent of roses filled the garden of *Hazeldene*. The sun shone down from a cloudless sky, warming the arms of the female guests in their light party dresses. A long table stood ready to receive the food still chilling in the fridges indoors. And on the patio, Maddy's father was in the process of making a speech.

His wife stood beside him, her smile alternating between embarrassment and pleasure. 'And then there was the time we had a bat fly into someone's bedroom,' he was saying. 'You could hear the screams all the way to Derby!'

Maddy saw several of the guests shudder, and she leant closer to David, his arm resting around her waist. She wore a plain dress, which fell to her calves in an elegant sweep of fabric. It was a linen mix, Inez had explained.

Lovely to wear, but resisting creases. The colour was something between a blue and a green, like the sea on a fine summer's day.

'And there was the incident when Lillian set fire to the kitchen curtains, lighting the candles on a birthday cake,' her father continued.

'I bet that was a pretty hot party,' whispered David.

Maddy gave him an affectionate poke in the ribs. 'Stop it.'

Her father was now thanking everyone who'd worked at *Hazeldene*. Fran and her sister were there. Georgie and her student friends. Plus so many others whom Maddy had known for as long as she could remember. 'And thanks also to those who came to our rescue when my precious wife, Lillian, was in hospital,' Mr Hope went on. 'I'm sure you'll agree how wonderful it is to see her glowing with health again.'

Applause rippled through the crowd as Lillian smiled and waved. 'We're particularly grateful to our daughter,

Maddy. She's made us so proud by setting up her shop on the High Street, *A Romantic Affair*. Mention *Hazeldene* and she'll give you a ten per cent discount.'

Maddy flinched. 'What's he trying to do — ruin me?'

But her father was into his stride now. 'As you know, an old friend of ours, David Reid, will be taking over *Hazeldene* shortly. He's going to close for a while, but when the place reopens it'll have a fabulous new restaurant. I hope you'll come along and try it out.' Mr Hope laughed to himself as David stretched up a hand in acknowledgement. 'I bet he'll give you a ten per cent discount too!'

'What?' David exclaimed.

'And finally, I have a surprise for Lillian. We agreed to take a holiday for the last fortnight of July before we move into the bungalow. But up until now, Lillian hasn't known where we're going.' He looked at his wife, waiting in nervous anticipation. 'As you know, this is our pearl wedding anniversary. And someone gave me a hint that Lillian has ambitions to take a cruise.'

He winked at Maddy. 'So I'm happy to announce that we'll be setting sail on the ship Sea Pearl, for a voyage up the Norwegian fjords.'

Lillian Hope gasped in delight and put her hands to her cheeks as another round of applause followed.

'Thank goodness for that,' murmured David. 'I thought he was going to say he was taking her pearl diving in the Pacific. They'd never have got travel insurance.'

'Oh, David,' chided Maddy. He could be so unromantic sometimes.

'My husband forgot to say that food will be served shortly,' Maddy's mother called out. 'So please just mingle for a while and help yourselves to more champagne.'

'I think we can manage that,' David said, taking Maddy's hand.

They walked across the lawn, stopping for a word with Guy and Inez, who were trying to spot the frogs in the pond. When they reached the fence, they turned to look back at *Hazeldene*.

For all its faults it was still such a fine old building. What adventures Maddy had enjoyed growing up there. It had given her quite an education seeing the guests troop through. The quirky ones, the rude ones. The ones with odd diets and the ones who claimed to be married, but so obviously weren't. At least, not to each other.

'Remember when the pipes burst and we were knee deep in water,' she said to David, to stop herself from dwelling on the fact that this felt like the end of an era.

'And the times you conscripted the guests' children into your dressing up games,' he said fondly. 'Didn't you ruin a pair of your mother's net curtains trying to make a wedding dress? Must have been one of your earlier attempts.'

They'd known one another so long now that she didn't even resent him reminding her. Getting to know David was like rediscovering something familiar; half forgotten. That serious young boy was now a man of calm intelligence whose strength she'd come to love. He was still unreadable. But then if she knew what he was thinking every minute, wouldn't she be bored?

'When we were in Australia and everything was going wrong, this was the place I used to remember,' David continued. 'It was the kind of hotel I dreamt of owning. I never imagined I'd be this lucky. *Hazeldene*'s always felt like it has a real heart.' He brushed her forehead with his lips.

'Yes,' Maddy agreed, a lump in her throat. 'But it can't be a museum. And your plans sound fantastic. Opening the restaurant, and converting those out-buildings into holiday cottages. And having a proper drying room for guests to leave their walking boots.'

'So you won't keep tripping over them,' he added, gripping her fingers more tightly in his warm, safe hand.

She gave him a curious glance. 'Me?'

He looked down at her with his familiar melting smile and stroked his thumb across her cheek. 'You know the kind of vision I have for *Hazeldene*. Come and share it with me.'

'Are you offering me a partnership?' she frowned. 'Like you have with Archie?'

'A kind of partnership, perhaps,' he grimaced, his dark eyes twinkling. 'But not like I have with Archie. Come back here as my wife.'

She caught her breath and looked away. 'David . . . ' She trailed off, unable to believe what he'd just asked her. Was there any man alive who'd put her through the turmoil David had? Or indeed, any who knew her so well, or whose presence made her feel so joyful and cared for?

'Two months and a lifetime,' he said. 'That's how long I've loved you.'

'Oh . . . OK,' she stammered. 'I mean, yes.'

And David bent to kiss her just as a fresh batch of champagne corks shot into the bright sky above *Hazeldene*.

We do hope that you have enjoyed reading this large print book.

Did you know that all of our titles are available for purchase?

We publish a wide range of high quality large print books including:
Romances, Mysteries, Classics
General Fiction
Non Fiction and Westerns

Special interest titles available in large print are:
The Little Oxford Dictionary
Music Book, Song Book
Hymn Book, Service Book

Also available from us courtesy of Oxford University Press:
Young Readers' Dictionary
(large print edition)
Young Readers' Thesaurus
(large print edition)

For further information or a free brochure, please contact us at:
Ulverscroft Large Print Books Ltd.,
The Green, Bradgate Road, Anstey,
Leicester, LE7 7FU, England.
Tel: (00 44) 0116 236 4325
Fax: (00 44) 0116 234 0205

Other titles in the
Linford Romance Library:

SOME EIGHTEEN SUMMERS

Lillie Holland

After eighteen years living a sheltered life as a vicar's daughter in Norfolk, Debbie Meredith takes work as a companion to the wealthy Mrs Caroline Dewbrey in Yorkshire. Travelling by train, she meets the handsome and charming Hugh Stacey. However, before long, Debbie is wondering why Mrs Dewbrey lavishes so much attention on her. And what of her son Alec's stance against her involvement with Hugh? Debbie then finds that she's just a pawn embroiled in a tragic vendetta . . .

THE GIRL FROM YESTERDAY

Teresa Ashby

Robert Ashton and Kate Gibson are a month away from their wedding. However, Robert's ex-wife Caroline turns up from Australia with a teenage daughter, Karen, who Robert knew nothing about. Then, as Caroline and Robert spend time together, they still seem to have feelings for one another, despite the fact that Jim, back in Australia, has asked Caroline to marry him. Now, Robert and Caroline must decide whether their futures lie with each other — or with Kate and Jim.

LOVERS NEVER LIE

Gael Morrison

Stacia Roberts has always played it safe, yet, longing for adventure, she travels to Greece expecting sunshine and excitement — and gets more than she'd ever bargained for. When strangers try to kill her, she suspects her fellow traveller Andrew Moore might be the enemy — but is he really a friend? Andrew blames himself for his wife's death. Then he falls in love with Stacia, vowing to keep her safe, a difficult task when he discovers she's an international thief.